AF236142

E. Rask, H. Lund

A short practical and easy method of Learning the Old Norsk Tongue or Icelandic Language

SALZWASSER
VERLAG

E. Rask, H. Lund

A short practical and easy method of Learning the Old Norsk Tongue or Icelandic Language

1st Edition | ISBN: 978-3-75250-522-1

Place of Publication: Frankfurt am Main, Germany

Year of Publication: 2020

Salzwasser Verlag GmbH, Germany.

Reprint of the original, first published in 1869.

A SHORT

PRACTICAL AND EASY METHOD

OF LEARNING THE

OLD NORSK TONGUE

OR

ICELANDIC LANGUAGE

AFTER THE DANISH

OF

E. RASK

WITH AN ICELANDIC READER
AN ACCOUNT OF THE NORSK POETRY AND THE SAGAS
AND A MODERN ICELANDIC VOCABULARY FOR TRAVELLERS

BY

H. LUND.

SECOND CORRECTED EDITION.

LONDON:

FRANZ THIMM,

FOREIGN BOOKSELLER AND PUBLISHER

24 LATE 3. BROOK STREET, GROSVENOR SQUARE W.

1869.

PREFACE.

The Old Norsk or Icelandic and the Anglo-Saxon may be termed the parents of the English Language, and their Knowledge is not only highly useful but absolutely necessary to every educated Englishman who looks upon his language with the eye of a historian and philosopher. Nothing is more interesting than to look back to these two sources from whence the english tongue is derived, and a thorough knowledge of English is only possible by being acquainted with its origin.

These languages together with Anglo-Norman, early German, ancient, mediæval and modern English, ought to be regularly studied.

By adapting Rask's abridgement we have indicated a simple method of learning Icelandic, which we hope will be found generally useful.

The Editor.

INDEX.

PART I.

The Pronunciation.

The Alphabet.

The Icelandic Alphabet is composed of the following letters

		Pronunciation				Pronunciation
A	a	ah		R	r	err
B	b	bay		S	s	s
D	d	day		T	t	tay
E	e	a		U	u	oo
F	f	eff		V	v	vay
G	g	gʰay		X	x	iks
H	h	hah		Y	y	ue
I	i	e		Z	z	zet
J	j	yod		Þ	þ	th
K	k	kah		Ð	ð	dh
L	l	el		Æ	æ	ae
M	m	em		Œ	œ	oe (Danish ø, Ger-
N	n	en				man ö)
O	o	o		Ö	ö	oe (German ö)
P	p	pay				

1. The Old Norsk order of the vowels was the following

Vowels		Diphthongs	
a		á	æ
ö		au	ey
e		—	ei
i		—	í
o		ó	œ
u		ú	—
y		—	ý

2. *ŏ* always open, as in the danish words: *Dŏren, lŏnne*.

3. *e*, the same as in the danish: *bedre, Hest*. Before the open *e* (*ε*) an *j* is often added in the pronunciation, which generally receives the accent (`) as: *lèt* (*ljet*) *lod*, agreeing with the Danish *sjette* from *seks*, *jèg* from *èγώ*. It is uncertain how far back into past ages this pronunciation may be traced.

4. *i*, as in the danish *vis, til*, it comes near to the danish *é* in *leve*, and is both long and short. When it goes over into *i*, it sounds like the danish in *Pil; vĭs, fire*.

5. *o*, always open, as the danish *â*, it is both long and short, as in: *Bogen, os, komme*; whilst *ó* sounds like the danish in *Os, Stol, stor*, perhaps à little broader.

6. *u* as in the danish words *Bud, Hul, kun*, long and short, ĭn its transition to *ù* it sounds like the danish *Hus, Hul, brun*. That this pronunciation of the *ŭ* and *ú* is the genuine old norsk, is proved not only by all the northern languages, but also by the Ferroe dialect, in which the correct sound has been maintainted to this day, f. i.

oldnorsk-ferroè		danish
kúnna		kunne
kúga	kùa	kùe.

7. *y* as in the danish *Byg, hyppe*; it approaches a little to the danish *ø* and is both long and short; changed into *ý* it sounds like the danish *Bly, Syre, flyde*. That *y* was really distinguished from *i*, is proved partly by the languages of the northern continent (Fastlands sprogene) partly by the icelandic pronunciation of the day, which pronounces *y* in *kyrr* short, but the letter *ý* long: but more particularly by the circumstance, that the poets (skaldene) form a half-rhyme with *i*, as Fms. 6, 35.

> Herstillis þarf ek hylli,
> hálf eru völd und Kálfi

8. *á* like the danish *av* in *Havre*, greek, latin and italian *au* in *aura* with a clear *a* (not like the german *au*).

9. *æ* almost like *aj*, so that the sound of *a* approaches the danish *æ*, and the sound of *j* somewhat resembles *e* (næsten *æje*.

10. *au*, as the danish *ŏw* or *ow*, which is still the pronunciation of the northern *au*, it is very much like the german *au*: *Auga*, Auge, the eye.

11. *ey*, as written, somewhat like *öj*, on northern monuments (Mindesmærker) it was often written *øy*, resembling the german *eu*. That it was distinguished from *ei* is partly seen from the Ferroe in which *ey* is changed into *oj*, *ei* into *aj*, but more particularly from the old verses, in which *ey* with *ei* form a half-rhyme as: Fms. 7, 13.

> hvern Þeirra kvað hærra
> (hjaldr-bliks) en sik miklu
> (beið ofmikit *ey*ðir
> ángr) makligra at hánga.

12. *ei* like a broad *é*, in conjunction with *i* (or *j*) the *e* loses its open sound and adopts the close one, in which the sound of *j* is but little heard, on this account this diphthong has sometimes been written *é* (not the german *ei*).

i and *ó* (see 4 et 5).

13. œ (ø) like a broad danish *ø* as pronounced by the people — *i Tø* —; the *j* sound becomes faint and ends almost with *e* (as in *øje*).

In many good and ancient icelandic manuscripts this sound is blended (foreblandet) with *æ*, and in the modern icelandic language œ (oe) has regularly changed into *æ* (ae); in Ferroe it has changed into *ø*, as: sœkja (søkja) ferroe: søkja, søje.

ú and *ý* (see 6 et 7).

14. The simple vowels, *a*, *ö*, *o*, *u* are hard *e*, *i*, *y*, soft after *g*, *k*; the diphthongs formed with *v* are hard, as: *á*, *au*, *ö*, *ú*; those formed with *j*, are soft; as: *œ*, *ey*, *ei*, *i*, *œ*, *y*. f. i. k a n n, k ö t t r, k o m a, k u n n a; also: k á l, k a u p, k o l, k ú g a; but: k e n n i, k i r k j a, k y r k i; and: k æ r t, k e y p t, k e i p r, k í f, k œ l i, k ý r.

15. The order of the Consonants is the following:

1) soundless (silent) Consonants:

	Labial letter	lingual letter	palatal letter
hard	p, f,	t, þ,	k, h,
soft	b, v,	d, ð,	g, j;

2) liquids:

	m, n,	l, r,	s, z.

3) mixed:

> x (z)

Of their pronunciation is to be remarked:

16. *f* has a double sound, namely 1) like *f* in the be-

ginning and when it is doubled, as in: fara, frá, vaff. 2)
like a hard *v* in all other cases, as: haf, nafn, höfn,
stefni, as seen in the Ferroe: *Navn, Hövn, stevni, stevndi,
stevnt.*

17. Þ (*th*) sounds like the english *th* in *think, thought.*
It is only found at the beginning of a word, and is therefore
never doubled. ð (*dh*) sounds almost like the *d* in the danish
words: *med, Bad, Råd,* most like the english *th* in: *bathe,
father*; it is heard more strongly rolling than other Consonants
as in: aðrir, öðlast, feðrum, riðnir, faðmar. It does
not appear at the beginning of words and never doubles, but
it changes indo *dd,* as: gleð = gladdi, ryð = ruddi.
The Ancients often wrote þ for ð, if the sense expressed its
meaning, but they never wrote *d* for ð before the 14th Century.

18. *k* has 1) the hard sound as in the danish *kan,* 2)
the soft sound (*kj*) as in *kært* (14) but never aspirated as in
the swedish *känner;* nor has *sk* the aspirated sound as in the
swedish *skär* or in the german word *Scheere,* but it is pronounced like the danish *skaere.*

19. *g* has 1) the hard sound as in *går;* 2) the soft (*gj*)
as in the danish *Gær* (14); 3) an aspirated sound after vowels or at the end of words or syllables, as the danish *g* in
Sag, Røg etc. We recognise this from the fact that the Ancients
always wrote in such cases *gh,* as: lögh, vegh. But it never
sounded like *j,* not even when followed by *i,* this is visible in
the old verses, in which otherwise the half-rhyme would have
either been corrupted or vanished altogether, as: Fms. 6, 23. 88.

eig-i gaztu liðskost *lág*-an ...
sýg ek or söltum *æg-i* ...

20. *h* is sounded at the beginning of words, also before
j. v, l, r, n, as: hjarta, hvat, hleð, hríng, hnoða.

21. *nn,* has a very peculiar hard sound after diphthongs,
like *dn,* as: steinn (steidn) fránn, kœnn, húnn; but not
if *nn* is joined to diphthongs as a compound, as: á-nni,
kú-nni, in such a case and after single vowels *nn* is pronounced as usual.

22. *ll* has a similar hard pronunciation after all vowels
and diphthongs, and sounds like *dl,* as: kall, áll, ill, fíll,
full, fúll; but it loses a great deal of its hardness when
followed by *t, d, s,* as: allt, felldi, fulls.

23. *rn* sounds very hard and short, almost like *dn* or more correctly like *rdn*, as: barn, börn, horn, it is therefore often found in defective modern manuscripts or books *steirn, seirn* for steinn, seinn. *rl* sounds likewise hard and short, almost like *dl* or more correctly like *rdl*; on this account one often finds jarl and jall, karl and kall, kerling and kelling.

24. *s* is always hard, like the Danish or like the german ß (*sz*), never soft like the german ſ.

25. *z* always sounds like *s* and is only used as an etymological sign for *s*, when a *t, d,* or ð has dropped as: veizla for *veitsla*, íslenzkr for *íslendskr*, gerzkr for *gerðskr*. In old manuscripts they made use of *z* sometimes as an abbreviation of *ss*, sometimes of *st*, about in the same manner in which the greek ζ stood for σð, in modern and good editions the use has been restricted, to specify distinctly the two pronunciations and derivations.

26. *x* always sounds hard, like *ks* or *gs* with a hard *g* and *s*, as: lax, sex, öx, uxi, (never like *gz* as in the french word *exact*).

27. The old Norsk pronunciation was altogether broad, rich in sound (klangfuld) logical and precise. A vowel before a simple consonant is rather long, whether the consonant be hard or soft, as: ek (l. æk) or eg (l. æg), set (l. sæt), las (l. lās) to express the short sound, the consonant is doubled, as: egg, sett, hlass.

Even vowels are shortened in the pronunciation if a consonant is added, as:

höf-uð has a long ö — höfði a short and sharp one.
ber, *slår* - - - e — berja, Dat. barði, has a short one.
vil   - - - i — vilja, vildi   - - - -

28. To the syllable belong all consonants which follow a vowel, as: ask-a, sett-u, höfð-in-u, vild-i, marg-ir, hest-ar. According to this rule the words are abbreviated at the end of a line.

29. Exceptions are *j* and *v*, which belong to the vowel following these letters, as: legg-jum, högg-va, the letter *r*, also never attaches itself to the preceding vowel, except, when it becomes altogether blended with the vowel as: steinn, grænn, hæll, fúll, it is generally read with the next vowel, as: veð-rit, veð-ŕ, al-ŕ, set-ŕ; such an r will always in future be thus accented ŕ.

30. The principal accent is constantly on the first syllable of the word as: vĕr-ald-ar-inn-ar; the secondary accent, lies on the penultimate in words of three or four syllables as: Upp-lend-íng-ar, vín-átta, svārāði, not on the last syllable, except in composed words, ending in a monosyllabic: konúngson.

II.

Modification of Vowels.

The Modification of vowels plays an important part in the declension and derivation of the Old Norsk Language. It is of a double kind.

31. a) *a* into *ð* in the principle syllable of a word if it ends in *u*, as: aska, ösku. Sometimes even if *u* is dropped as: blað, Plural blöð, leaves. Jafn, jöfn. Reversed:

32. *ð* into *a*, if the termination be *a*, as: ögn, agnar, sometimes before *ir* or with shortened terminations in compounds or derivations, as: agnir, jarðvegŕ, jarðneskŕ.

33. b) Before endings in *i*, *j*, or *r*, even if these letters are left out:

a into *e*:	land, lendi	— nafn, nefni;
ð — *e*:	gröf, gef	— sök, sekr;
ja — *i*:	bjart, birti	— djarft, dirfist;
jð — *i*:	hjörð, hirðir	— björn, birni;
e — *i*:	regn, rignir	— hverfi, hvirfill;
á — *œ*:	ráð, ræðŕ	— ná. næ;
au — *ey*:	raun, reyni	— draup, dreypi;
o — *y*:	son, synir	— of, yfir;
u — *y*:	guð, gyðja	— full, fylli;
ú — *ý*:	hús, hýsi	— prútt, prýði;
jó — *ý*:	bjóða, býðŕ	— hljóð, hlýði;
jú — *ý*:	fljúga, flýgŕ	— djúpt, dýpra;
ó — *œ* (*œ*):	kló, klœr	— bót, bœti.

o sometimes, although rarely into *e*, as:

hnot, hnetr — troða, treðr;
koma, kemr — of, efra, efst.

34. In the oldest norsk language there were long and single vowels before *ng*, *nk*, these changed according to the above rule, as: langt, löngu, lengi, in latter times these vowels were modified into diphthongs and changed thus: lángt, laungu, leingi.

35. Sometimes there is no modification even if *i* follows, nor if even the vowel on other occasions is changed in its root, as: land, Dative landi; nafn, - nafni, and þánki, *thought* kappi, *fighter*, although: ek þeinki, *I think*, ek keppist, *I fight* are used. The reason of this appears to be that in such cases the vowel of the termination was not *i* but *e*, as we frequently find it in manuscripts thus: *lande, nafne, þanke, kappe.*

36. In the same way o is often found in terminations instead of *u*, particularly, so it appears, if the chief syllable received no modification of this kind, as: ero, váro, þíngom etc. But according to rule, there is a difference in such endings between *e* and *i*, *o* and *u*.

37. There are many kinds of modification in the conjugation of the verbs, which will be mentioned in the proper place.

38. Amongst the consonants change:

ndt into *tt* as: batt, *bandt*; satt, *sandt*.

ngk — *kk* — sprakk, *sprang*; ekkja, *Enke*.

39. *nr* into *nn* as: steinn, *steinr*; seinn, *seinr*; seinna, *sein-ra.*

lr into *ll*, as: hóll, for *hólr*, sælli for *sæl-ri.*

40. *v* is dropped at the beginning of words before *o, u, y* and *r*, as: verð, varð, urðu, yrði, orðit; as also: hverf, hvarf, hurfu, hyrfi, horfit; rángt, *vrangt*, reiði, *Vrede*, But we find that the Ancients frequently did not drop the *v*, as: vurðu, vyrði, vorðit.

Inflection of Words.

1. *The Noun.*

41. Nouns are divided into two orders, the *open* and the *closed;* the one is more simple in its inflection, the other more complex.

The first has but one declension, the second has two. Each has three genders. The Neuter is the most simple.

Open Order.

42. *First Declension.*

		the eye Neuter.	the sunbeam Masculine.	the tongue Feminine.
Sing.	*Nom.*	auga,	geisli,	túnga
Acc. Dat. Gen.		auga,	geisla,	túngu (o)
Plural	*Nom.*	augu (o),	geislar,	túngur (or),
	Acc.	augu (o),	geisla,	túngur (or),
	Dat.	augum (om),	geislum (om),	túngum (om),
	Gen.	augna	geisla	túngna

43. Nouns, whose chief letter is *a,* change *a* into *ö* before the terminations in *u* (31):

bjarta, *Plural, D.* hjörtum, (the heart)
kappi — - köppum, (the champion)
saga, *A. D. G.* sögu - sögur, sögum, (the saga)
on the other hand *a* changes into *u* in the following syllables, as: harpari, hörpurum; leikari, leikurum.

44. Some masculine substantives ending in *ingi,* take a *j* in all other cases, as:

höfðíngi, höfðingja, höfðingjar — the captain;
illvirki, illvirkja — the illdoer;
vili, vilja — will.

45. Masculines ending in *andi* form their plural irregularly, f. i. búandi, which word is at the same time contracted, as:

Sing.	*Nom.*	búandi (*the yeoman*)	bóndi, (e)
	Acc. Dat. Gen.	búanda	bónda,
Plur.	*Nom. Acc.*	búendr,	bœndr, bændr,
	Dat.	búöndum, -endum,	bóndum, bændum,
	Gen.	búanda, -enda	bónda, bænda.

46. The words h e r r a and s í r a (germ. Herr, english Sire, father) which were used before christian names of Priests and Provosts (*Sira Arni*, The Revd. Mr. Arne), are the only masculines ending in *a*, they only differ from g e i s l i in the Nominative.

47. Some Feminines take in the plural not -*na* but only -*a*, as in the Nom. Sing. as: l í n a, k a n n a, s k e p n a, l i l j a, g y ö j a, v a r a.

48. The subst. k o n a (Queen), *woman*, changes in the Gen. plural into k v e n n a (wife); the word k v i n n a remains sometimes in this case unchanged by ancient writers, the moderns always use k v e n n a.

Closed Order.

49. This Order embraces not only the words ending in consonants, but also those ending in *i* and *u*. Ten masculine substantives ending in *i* of the first Declension, ought to end in *e*.

This order is divided in two declensions, to the first belong the words ending in consonants and in *i*, to the second belong those ending in a pure sounding *u*.

50. *Second Declension.*

		N.	M.	F.
Sing.	*Nom.*	land (land)	brandŕ (brand)	för (journey)
	Acc.	land	brand	för
	Dat.	landi (e)	brandi (e)	för
	Gen.	lands	brands	farar
Plur.	*Nom.*	lönd	brandar	farir (ar)
	Acc.	lönd	branda	farir (ar)
	Dat.	löndum	bröndum	förum
	Gen.	landa	branda	fara.

51. When there is neither *a* nor *ö*, no modification occurs, as: s k i p (ship), s k i p u m — k o n ú n g ŕ (king), k o n ú n - g u m — e i g n (property), e i g n, e i g n a r, e i g n i r, e i g n u m. only one word has two forms, namely:

Sing. dagŕ (the day) *Dat.* degi,
Plur. dagar - dögum.

52. The letter *r* dissolves when *n* or *l* precede, into *nn* and *ll*, as in s t e i n n (the stone) instead of s t e i n ŕ, h æ l l (heel) instead of hælŕ, and in longer words as: d r o t t i n n (master).

lykill (key). Sometimes the *i* of the Dative drops in the words ending in *ll* as:

hæl, hól for hæli, hóli.

In the last radical letters *r* and *s* the use fluctuates between *r* and *rr*, *s* and *ss*. Þórr, herr, hauss, íss, óss, is often found because of little consequence.

Both kinds of words, if they are monosyllabic in the Nom. lose the *i* in the Dative, as: her, ís, for heri, ísi.

The *r* is altogether dropped after *n* and *l* when it comes into collision with other consonants as in: vagn, hrafn, fugl, karl (Nom. and Acc.) also after *s* and *ss*, as in háls, kross (in the Nom. Acc. and Gen.).

53. Words in two syllables are contracted when the pronunciation allows it, as:

Neut. sumar (summer), sumri — *Plur.* sumur sumrum, sumra.

höfuð (head), höfði, höfðum, höfða.

Masc. hamri, hamrar, hamra, hömrum

drottni, drottnar — lykli, lyklar etc.

Some words receive an uncommon vowel in the contracted forms, as:

megin, *might*, *power*; D. magni, G. megins. *Pl.* megin or mögn (as: goðmögn), D. mögnum, G. magna.

g. m. ketill (*kettle*), D. katli, *Plur.* katlar, A. katla, D. kötlum,

g. f. alin (*the ell-measure*) G. álnar, - álnir, álnum, álna

54. To the contracted belong the *Mascul.* jöfurr, fjöturr, they keep *ö* throughout jöfri, fjötri *Plur.* jöfrar, fjötrar.

The others of this class of all three genders have only an *r̂* by the ancient writers (not *ur* or *urr*), they must not therefore be looked upon as contracted, as:

Neu. silfr̂ (silver), silfri,

Mas. akr̂ (acre), akri, *Plur.* akrar,

Fem. fjöðr (feather) fjaðrar, *Plur.* fjaðrir (ar) fjöðrum, fjaðra.

55. The polysyllabic neuters ending in -að, -an or the *fem.* ending in *an* are not contracted, as:

Sing. Nóm. Acc. mannlíkan (*human being*)	skipan (*order*),
Dat. mannlíkani	skipan
Gen. mannlíkans	skipanar (-onar)
Plur. Nom. Acc. mannlíkun (on)	skipanir,
Dat. mannlíkunum (onum)	skipunum (onom)
Gen. mannlíkana	skipana.

56. Some words of this declension allow a *j* or *v* to creep in before terminations which begin with a vowel, not however *j* before *i*, rarely *v* before *u*. This seems to be a remnant of terminations in *i* or *u* which were originally in these words.

57. The inserted letter *v* protects a preceding *ŏ* (or *au*) from changing into *a* or *ā* (see § 32) if it terminates in *a* it has the same effect as *u*. In the Plural of the Fem. the inserted *v* takes the old termination in *ar*

Sing.	*Nom.*	frœ (fræ)	saungr̃	ŏr
	Acc.	frœ	saung	ŏr
	Dat.	frœvi	saungvi	ŏru (ŏr)
	Gen.	frœs	saungs	ŏrvar
Plural	*Nom.*	frœ	saungvar	ŏrvar
	Acc.	frœ	saungva	ŏrvar
	Dat.	frœvum (om)	saungum (om)	ŏrum (om)
	Gen.	frœva;	saungva;	ŏrva.

58. The inserted letter *j* requires the Masculine to drop the entire termination (*ji*) in the Sing. Dat. and to take in the plural *ir* Acc. *i*. but the feminine always takes the *ar*, so that it terminates in *jar*, as;

Sing.	*Nom.*	nes (*neck of land*)	dreingr̃	ben (*wound*)
	Acc.	nes	dreing	ben
	Dat.	nesi	dreing	ben
	Gen.	ness	dreings	benjar
Plural	*Nom.*	nes	dreingir	benjar
	Acc.	nes	dreingi	benjar
	Dat.	nesjum	dreingjum	benjum
	Gen.	nesja;	dreinja;	benja.

59. But there are a number of masculines with simple vowels or consonants before *r̃*, which also drop the *i* in the Sing. Dat. who take in the Nom. and Acc. Plur. *ir*, and *i* without inserting *j* — equally a number of fem. ending in –*ing*, –*ung* or in *r̃* (or *i*) which take *ar* in the plural without the insertion of either *v* or *j* as: [*hunt*]

Sing.	*Nom.*	dal'r (*dale*)	drottning (*queen*)	veiðr (veiði) (*chase,*
	Acc.	dal	drottning	veiði
	Dat.	dal	drottningu	veiði
	Gen.	dals	drottningar	veiðar
Plur.	*Nom.*	dalir	drottningar	veiðar
	Acc.	dali	drottningar	veiðar
	Dat.	dŏlum	drottningum	veiðum
	Gen.	dala;	drottninga;	veiða.

But *dali* is sometimes found in the Dat. (f. i. Harbarðsl. 18) even in the Plur. *Herdalar* (Hk. 2, 8) likewise in the swedish; brúðr̃ has in the Plural brúðir.

60. Some words resemble the third declension as they terminate in the Sing. Gen. in *ar*, otherwise they are declined like brandr̃, dreingr̃ or dalr̃. To the former belong: hattr̃, kraptr̃ (kraftr̃) grautr̃, skógr̃, vindr̃ in the language of the old bards vegr̃. To the latter belong: belgr̃, mergr̃, leggr̃, hryggr̃, verkr̃, reykr̃, lækr̃, drykkr̃ and bœr, therefore: bœjar, bœjum, bœja with inserted *j*, which is strictly observed by all good ancient authors; of the latter kind are mostly found: staðr̃, sauðr̃, bragr̃, vegr̃ (sometimes in the Acc. vegu), rèttr̃, vinr̃ (or vin) hugr̃, hlutr̃, munr̃ (difference) and all those ending in *-naðr̃* (*-nuðr*) and *-skapr*, which occur however rarely in the plural.

61. The neuter terminating in *-i*, and the masc. terminating in *-ir*, drop the *i* before the terminations: *-um, -ar, -a*, except those having *g* or *k* before them, these change *i* into *j*.

The feminine ending in a pure *i* remains unchanged in Sing. but takes *ir* in the Plural:

Sing. Nom.	kvæði	merki	læknir	æfi
Acc. Dat.	kvæði	merki	lækni	æfi
Gen.	kvæðis	merkis	læknis	æfi
Plur. Nom.	kvæði	merki	lækn-ar	æfir
Acc.	kvæði	merki	lækn-a	æfir
Dat.	kvæð-um	merkjum	lækn-um	æf-um
Gen.	kvæð-a;	merkja;	lækn-a;	æf-a.

Eyrir (Danish: *en Øre*) an ear, forms the plural in
aurar
aura | but eyri a low beach, has in the
aurum | Gen. Plural eyrar.
aura

helgi, *holiness*, *holiday*, *Sunday*, forms Gen. Plur. helgar.

62. Others again from all three genders have many irregularities. Thus the neuter læti, sound, forms Dat. Plur. látum, Gen. láta. Some neuters become feminine in the Plural, as:

Singular:	*Plural:*
lim, *brushwood*	limar, *branches*,
tál, *fraud*	tálar, *frauds*,
eing (Dan. en Eng) *meadow*	eingjar, *meadows*,
mund, *time*	mundir, *times*,
þúsund (Dan. Tusende) *thousand*	þúsundir, *thousands*.

The word frœði, *knowledge*, is in the Singular feminine
and remains unchanged, like æfi; but in the Plural it is
neuter and is declined like kvæði.

63. Some neuters are found in the Nom. and Acc. with
and without the termination in -*i*, as: eing and eingi;
fullting (Dan. Hjœlp) *help*; and fulltingi; sinn, and
sinni, the longer form belongs to the modern icelandic
language, but often appears in modern copies of old manuscripts.

64. The Masculine guð, which drops the *r* in the Nom.
and forms the Plur. in guðir, is distinguished from the Neuter
goð (heathen image) Plur. goð. Many words ending in *i*
and *r* form the Plur. in -*ar*, as:

kærleikr, kærleik, or kærleiki, kærleika;
Plural kærleikar.

sannleikr, sannleiki; *Plural* sannleikar.

The forms -*leiki* are common in the modern language. The
new form often gives a new signification as:

oddr, *a point*, oddi — *a neck of land;*
munnr (Dan. Mund) *mouth* — munni, *mouth of river;*
karl, *an old man* — Karli, *male name „Charles".*

Some differ altogether:

bragr (= staðr 60) *a poem* — Bragi, *male name;*
hugr, *will* — hugi, *sense, thought* and male name *Hugo;*
hlutr, *an ounce, thing* — hluti, *a part.*

It happens sometimes that words are similar to these terminations, without being related together, as:

bolr (= dalr) *block* — boli, *bull;*
hagr, *condition* — hagi, *garden,*

It is rare that the *neuter* of this declension changes into the
masc. of the former, by taking the termination of *i*; as:

ómak and ómaki (Gylfaginning 12) *fainting fit;*
mál, *speech* — formáli, *tale;*
verk, *work* — verki, *writing, poem,*

with the exception of those which lose at the same time their
entire signification, as:

land, *land* — landi, *countryman;*
bú (Dan. Bo), *furniture* — bui, *neighbour;*
höfuð (Dan. Hoved) *head* — höfði, *Cape;*
norðr (Dan. Norden) *north* — Norðri, *name of a dwarf.*

65. The other irregular Masculines are:

Sing.	*Nom.*	skór (*shoe*)	dörr (*spear*)	maðr (*man*)	fing'r (*finger*)
	Acc.	skó	dör	mann	fíng'r
	Dat.	skó	dör	manni	fingri
	Gen.	skós	dörs	manns	fing'rs
Plur.	*Nom.*	skúar	derir	menn	fing'r
	Acc.	skúa	deri	menn	fing'r
	Dat.	skóm	dörum	mönnum	fingrum
	Gen.	skúa;	darra;	manna;	fingra.

The moderns contract skór in the Plural Nom. skór, Acc. skó, Gen. skóa.

66. Irregular feminines are:

sál, *the soul,* Dat. sálu — *Plural* sálir, Gen. sálna, also in the Gen. *Sing.* sálu, particularly found in compounds, as: sáluhjálp.

grein forms the Plural in greinir and sometimes greinar, ey, island, Dat. eyju or ey, *Plur.* eyjar — now eya is generally used in Iceland after the 1st Declension. Monosyllables ending in á, which come in contact with an a or u following, generally supplant them by á, as: brá, *eyebrow,* Gen. brár, *Plur.* brár, Dat. brám, Gen. brá. Some derivatives with these endings remain unaltered in the Sing. by the ancients as: ásjá, *care.*

Third Declension.

67. This declension embraces all those words ending in u or v, which are however frequently dropped or in some other manner obscured. There are but few neuters, all of which end in e (for ev), the Masc. end in the Sing. in -ar, Plur. -ir, Fem. of the Sing. in -ar, or -r, form the Plural in -r:

		N.	M.		F.	[(*wood*)
Sing.	*Nom.*	tre (*tree*)	völlur (*field*)	fjörður (*bay*)	rót (*root*)	mörk
	Acc.	tre	völl	fjörð	rót	mörk
	Dat.	tre	velli	firði	rót	mörk
	Gen.	tres	vallar	fjarðar	rótar	merk'r
Plur.	*Nom.*	tre	vellir	firðir	rœt'r	merk'r
	Acc.	tre	völlu	fjörðu	rœt'r	merk'r
	Dat.	trjám	völlum	fjörðum	rótum	mörkum
	Gen.	trjá;	valla;	fjarða;	róta;	marka.

68. Like tre are declined kne; two words hle and spe do not occur in the Plural. It was only in the fifteenth Century that the Icelanders began to pronounce the *e* in these words like *je* (instead of *æ*) wherefore we meet in good editions of old works the reading trè, très etc. Plur. Dat. and Gen. contracted for trjavum, trjava.

The word fe, *cattle, goods, money*, is irregular in the Gen. Sing.; we find fjár instead of fjavar; but ve, *sanctuary, temple* (from which Oðinsve, *Odense*) is declined, like land or skip after the 2nd Declension.

69. The Masculines we find sometimes only written with *r* (instead of *ur*), it not being observed that the termination in *u* was the reason for writing *ð*, as in the Dat. Plural.

Therefore hvalŕ with *a*, because the *r* is only distinguished by an ' from the root.

But kjölur with *ð*, because the ending contains *u*. The Accus. Plural of all these words has a double form, partly ending in *i*, agreeing with the Nom. Plural as: velli, firði, partly ending in -*u*, agreeing with the Dative Plural, and this form is the old genuine one. Several kinds of modifications are to be noticed, although some words do not modify by reason of their nature.

Sing.	*Nom.*	sonur (*son*)	dráttur (*drawing*)	viður (*wood, forest*)
	Acc.	son	drátt	við
	Dat.	syni	drætti	viði
	Gen.	sonar	dráttar	viðar
Plur.	*Nom.*	synir	drættir	viðir
	Acc.	(syni)	(drætti)	(vidi)
	—	sonu	dráttu	viðu
	Dat.	sonum	dráttum	viðum
	Gen.	sona;	drátta;	viða.

Irregular are these two:

Sing.	*Nom.*	fótur (*foot*)	vet'r (*for* vetr-ur) (*winter*)
	Acc.	fót	vet'r (*for* vetr-u)
	Dat.	fœti	vetri
	Gen.	fótar	vetrar
Plur.	*Nom. Acc.*	fœtŕ	vet'r (*for* vetr-'r)
	Dat.	fótum	vetrum
	Gen.	fóta;	vetra.

70. The feminines of this declension have also several kinds of modification of vowels; some cannot be modified, some have a doubled form of declension after this or the former specimen, as:

		Present Declension:		*Former Declension*: [*stock*)	
Sing. Nom. Acc.	hnot(*nut*)	staung	mörk (*wood*)	staung (*stake,*
Dat.	hnot	staung	mörku	staung
Gen.	hnotar	-steingr	markar	stángar
Plur. Nom. Acc.	hnetr	steingr	markir	stángir
Dat.	hnotum	staungum	mörkum	staungum
Gen.	hnota;	stánga;	marka;	stánga.

The modification in s t a u n g, s t e i n g̊r is in reality the same, as in m ö r k, m e r k̊r (67) as it is merely a mechanical consequence of *ng*, the *ö* changes into *au* and *e* into *ei*, we also often find s t ö n g, s t a n g a r, s t e n g̊r (34).

The words which are declined in two ways like m ö r k and s t a u n g are chiefly the following:

s t r ö n d (*strand*), r ö n d (*edge*) s p a u n g, t a u n g, h a u n k.

A difference of signification is only accidental, as:

ö n d, *Plur.* e n d̊r *the duck* — ö n d, *Plur.* a n d i r, *a spirit, ghost* (dan.: e n Å n d.)

S t r ö n d, r ö n d, ö n d receive in the *Gen. Sing.* always s t r a n - d a r, r a n d a r, a n d a r; so that ö n d, *spirit*, differs only in one case in the singular, and two cases in the Plural from ö n d, *duck*, *Dat. Sing.* ö n d u, Nom. and Acc. *Plur.* a n-d i r.

71. Some accented monosyllables deviate by contraction, if the final syllable begins with a vowel, so that *á* absorbs *a, u* but *ó, ú*, absorbs only the *u*; as:

t á, *ten*, G. t á r (for t á a r) — *Plur.* t æ r, *D.* t á m (for t á u m)
k l o, *claw*, G. k l ó a r — *Plur.* k l œ r, k l ó m, k l ó a
á, *sheep* (hunfâr), *Gen.* — *Plur.* æ r.
k-ú *row*, G. k ý r — *Plur.* k ý r.

These forms æ r and k ý r we find in the modern language given to the Sing. Nom.; so that both these words are in the Sing. Nom. and Plur. Nom. and Acc. the same.

Others blend the *r* of the Plural with the final letter, as b r ú n, *Plur.* b r ý n n (Egilss. S. 306 and in the Edda Hel-gakv. Haddsk. 19) now we say b r ý n, or b r ý r; m ú s forms the *Plur.* in m ý s s or m ý s; d y r r or d y r, *door*, is only found

in the Plural and forms the *Dat.* and *Gen.* durum, dura
or dyrum, dyra.

The following are still more irregular:

Sing. Nom. Acc.	hönd (*hand*)	nátt	*or*	nótt (*night*)
Dat.	hendi	nátt		nóttu
Gen.	handar	náttar		nætr (noetr)
Plur. Nom. Acc.	hendr	nætr		(noetr)
Dat.	höndum	náttum		nóttum
Gen.	handa;	nátta;		nótta.

72. Some of the names of relations ending in *-ir*, would
require a separate declension, if there were not so few,
namely:

		father	*brother*	*daughter*	*sister*
Sing.	*Nom.*	faðir	bróðir	dóttir	systir
Acc. Dat. Gen.		föður	bróður	dóttur	systur
Plur. Nom. Acc.		feðr	broeðr	doetr	systr
Dat.		feðrum	broeðrum	doetrum	systrum
Gen.		feðra;	broeðra;	doetra;	systra.

Like bróðir is declined móðir, *mother.*

We find in the Ancients the Dat. Sing. of faðir, feðr,
of bróðir, broeðr.

73. We also find in the Ancient language some peculiar
names of relatives with different terminations, which embrace
two and more persons in one name, and which occur therefore only in the plural; if the two persons are of different
genders, they are in the neuter:

> hjón, *man and woman;*
> systkin, *brother and sister;*
> hju, *youth and girl, or man and woman;*
> feðgin, *father and daughter;*
> moeðgin, *mother and son;*
> feðgar, *father and son;*
> moeðgur, *mother and daughter.*

To these belongs also börn, the only one which also occurs
in the Singular. barn (= land); only feðgar is masc. and
moeðgur, fem. (= túngur) Gen. moeðgna.

Declension of Nouns with the Article.

74. In the declension of the noun with the article hit, hinn, hin, both retain their endings unaltered, so that both combined have a double declension. The article is thus declined:

Sing.	*Nom.*	hit	hinn	hin
	Acc.	hit	hinn	hina
	Dat.	hinu	hinum	hinni
	Gen.	hins	hins	hinnar
Plur.	*Nom.*	hin	hinir	hinar
	Acc.	hin	hina	hinar
	Dat.		hinnum	
	Gen.		hinna	

The *h* is continually dropped when the article is compounded with a substantive ending in a short vowel, *a, i, u,* the *-i* is also dropped after every polysyllabic word ending in *-r*.

75. The substantives when used with the article drop the *m* of the Dative Plural, they end therefore in *u*, whilst the article drops *-hi*.

First Order.

Sing.	*Nom.*	hjarta-t (*heart*)	andi-nn (*spirit*)	gata-n (*road*)
	Acc.	hjarta-t	anda-nn	götu-na
	Dat.	hjarta-nu	anda-num	götu-nni
	Gen.	hjarta-ns	anda-ns	götu-nnar
Plur.	*Nom.*	hjörtu-n	andar-nir	götur-nar
	Acc.	hjörtu-n	anda-na	götur-nar
	Dat.	hjörtu-num	öndu-num	götu-num
	Gen.	hjartna-nna;	anda-nna;	gatna-nna

76. It must be borne in mind with respect to the 2nd and 3rd Order where the *i* in the Dat. of masc. subst. is wangtin they do not take the *i* of the Article either, as:

dreingr-inn, dreingnum; dalrinn, dalnum.

But those which can take an *i* keep it, as: ísinum, better than ísnum; stólinum (Snorra-Edda 114) better than stólnum.

77. Second Order.

		N.	M.	F.
Sing.	Nom.	skip-it (ship)	konúngr-inn (king)	eign-in (property)
	Acc.	skip-it	konúng-inn	eign-ina
	Dat.	skipi-nu	konúngi-num	eign-inni
	Gen.	skips-ins	konúngs-ins	eignar-innar
Plur.	Nom.	skip-in	konúngar-nir	eignir-nar
	Acc.	skip-in	konúnga-na	eignir-nar
	Dat.	skipu-num	konúngu-num	eignu-num
	Gen.	skipa-nna;	konúnga-nna;	eigna-nna.

78. The ř before a vowel is pronounced with it and loses its half sound, as: silf-rit, málm-rinn, fjöð-rin.

79. All the contracted and irregular forms remain as they are, as:

degi-num, katli-num, sálu-nni, álnar-innar;
ï retains its half-sound before n, as: bœndř-nir, fingř-na. Only maðř (65) adds in the Nom. Plur. -ïr. and in the Acc. -i, therefore: mennir-nir (rarely menninnir), menni-na.

80. The monosyllabic feminine often expels the hi of the article in the Acc. Sing. as:

för-na, instead of för-ina, gröfna inst. of gröf-ina (Snorra-Edda, 138); reið-na for reið-ina; húðna for húðina (Snorra-Edda 144).

81. In case the substantive be a monosyllable, ending in a long vowel or double sound (Tvelyd) the i of the article is retained if the word remains monosyllabic, but it is left out if the word becomes trisyllabic as:

skrá-in, skrá-na, skrá-nni;
ey-in, ey-na, ey-nni (thus also eyju-nni 66).

82. Third Order.

		N.	M.	F.
Sing.	Nom.	kne-ït (knee)	kjölr-inn (keel)	bók-in (book)
	Acc.	kne-ït	kjöl-inn	bók-ina
	Dat.	kne-nu	kili-num	bók-inni
	Gen.	knes-ins	kjalar-ins	bókar-innar
Plur.	Nom.	kne-ïn	kilir-nir	bœkř-nar
	Acc.	kne-ïn	kjölu-na	bœkř-nar
	Dat.	knjá-num	kjölu-num	bóku-num
	Gen.	knjá-nna;	kjala-nna;	bóka-una.

2*

83. The more modern form tr è ð for tr eꞮt is yet found in good manuscripts.

.84. On the whole the irregularities before the article remain as in the second Order, as: mýsnar, dyrnar, or in the Neuter dyrrin; but brýnnar, with two, not three *n* (Snorra-Edda 50) is used.

II. Adjectives.

85. The Adjective agrees much with the noun, but by no means in so perfect a manner as in greek or latin.

Joined to the article, which precedes the adjective, it makes an imperfect declension, which is termed the *„definite form“*, resembling the first order of the noun, only that its plural is much simpler, as it always ends in *u*, leaving to the article its further definition. Without an article the adjective has quite a different and perfect declension, which is termed the *„indefinite form“* resembling the closed form of the noun in its second declension. For there is no Adj. in which the Plur. n. g. ends in -*e*, or the m. g. Acc. Plur. in -*u*, or the f. g. Plur. in *ɼ*. This is the more primitive form and has therefore the precedent.

Both forms distinguish three genders, and they resemble therefore the six classes of the declension of the noun.

86. S p a k t may serve as a complete Paradigm:

Indefinite Form.

		N.	M.	F.
Sing.	*Nom.*	spak-t (*wise*)	spak-ɼ	spök
	Acc.	spak-t	spak-an	spak-a
	Dat.	spök-u	spök-um	spak-ri
	Gen.	spaks		spak-rar
Plur.	*Nom.*	spök	spak-ir	spak-ar
	Acc.	spök	spak-a	spak-ar
	Dat.		spökum	
	Gen.		spakra.	

Definite Form.

Sing.	Nom.	spaka	spaki	spaka
	Gen. Dat. Acc.	spaka	spaka	spöku

Plur.	Nom. Acc.		spöku	
	Dat.		spöku or spökum	
	Gen.		spöku.	

87. Although the adjective has but one declension there are several exceptions to be observed which occur through the joining of the final syllable with the root.

If the last radical letter be ð preceded by a vowel or a diphthong, it absorbs in the n. g. with *t* to *tt* as:

glatt, glaðr, glöð — *glossy, bright;*
breitt, breiðr, breið — *broad;*

in one case, the accent is lost, namely in

gott, góðr, góð (*good*).

If a consonant precedes, the ð is altogether dropped:

hart, harðr, hörð (*hard*) — sagt, sagðr, sögð (*said*)
haft, hafðr, höfð (*clever*)

The same in dissyllabic words, if a vowel precedes:

kallat, kallaðr, kölluð;
lagit, lagiðr, lagið (for kallaðt, lagiðt).

Also *d* after a consonant as:

vant, vandr, vönd (*difficult*) — selt, seldr, seld;
geymt, geymdr, geymd.
gladt, gladdr, glödd (*glad*) — breidt, breiddr,
breidd (*broad*) — mœdt, mœddr, mœdd (*tired*).

If the word ends in *tt,* no further *t* is added in the n. g. but the form becomes similar to the feminine, as:

sett, settr, sett — mœtt, mœttr, mœtt.

In weaker consonants the gender may part as: latt, lattr, lött, nor can it be distinguished in the n. g. from a similar word with single *t,* as:

latt, latr, löt (*lazy*) — hvatt, hvattr, hvött and
hvatt, hvatr, hvöt (*hasty*).

88. The adjectives, the root of which end in an accented vowel, deviate in so far that they double the -*t* in the n. g., the -*r* in the f. g. in the terminations -*ri* and -*rar*, the -*ra* in the Gen. Plur., and often the -*s* in n. and m. g. Gen. Sing. as

þrátt, þrár, þrá, þráss, þrárrar, þrárra;
auðsætt, auðsær, auðsæ (*clear*).

mjótt, mjór, mjó (*delicate, narrow*) — trútt, trúr,
trú (*true*)

nýtt, nýr, ný, nýss etc. (*new*)

Those with -*á*, are sometimes contracted if followed by *a* or *u*,
which are swallowed up by *á*, as:

blá for bláu — blán for bláan — blám for bláum.

Likewise in the definite form, as:

hinn grái, *Acc.* hinn grá, *Dat.* hinum grá, *Gen.* hins
grá. The contracted forms belong to the modern Icelandic
and are scarcely written in old Manuscripts. The ancient language therefore sometimes inserts *f* (or *v*) to escape the contraction, as:

hátt, hár, há (*high*) — m. g. *Acc.* háfan, *Dat.* háfum,
háfom (or hám); def. form háfa, háfi, háfa, háfu.
mjófa, mjófan, mjófum; def. form mjófa, mjófi etc.

The word nýtt inserts *j* before all vowels, with the exception
of *i*, as: nýju, nýjan.

89. Some adjectives insert *j* or *v* after the last consonant, without altering the declension, these resemble the
nouns in 57 and 58, as:

dökkt (dökt), dökkr, dökk (*dark*);
Plur. dökk, dökkvir (döcqvir), dökkvar;
Def. form: dökkva, dökkvi, dökkva.

The only adjective which inserts *j* correctly is:

mitt, miðr, mið — therefore:
miðjan, miðja, miðju, miðjum, miðri.

In some words the last radical letter of which is *g* or *k*,
a *j* is sometimes inserted before *a* or *u*, as:

frægt, frægr, fræg; *Acc.* frægan or frægjan; *Dat.*
frægum or frægjum.
sekr, sekan or sekjan.

90. Monosyllables ending in *r* after a long vowel or diphthong are regular, as:

ber-t, ber-r, ber; fœr-t, fœr-r, fœr.

The masculine termination -*r* is dropped in modern Icelandic,
as the pronunciation has changed and the m. g. and f. g.
have become the same in the Nom.

Those words whose vowels are short, and have therefore a double *r*, drop one *r* in the n. g., before -*t* and before the termination to satisfy the orthography as three *r's* ought not to appear; but such words retain the double *r* in the f. g. Nom.; as otherwise the vowels would be long and the root deformed. As: þurt, þurr, þurr (*dry*); kyrt, kyrr, kyrr (*still*). Those ending in *s*, agree with this rule, as: laust, lauss, laus (*free*); particularly as a diphthong precedes; but hvast, hvass, hvöss (not hvös) because the vowel is short.

In a word with a double *s* the vowel is accented in the n. g. as: víst, viss, viss.

91. If a consonant precedes the last radical letter *r*, it changes before -*t* and *s* into ' (halfsound), never into *ur*; but into *r* before a vowel and the terminations -*rí, rar, ra*, one of the *r* is dropped, as a double *r* behind a consonant cannot be pronounced. The following example will prove the force of these observations:

Sing. Nom.	fagrt	fagr'	fögr' (*for* fög-ru)	
Acc.	fagrt	fagran	fagra	
Dat.	fögru	fögrum	fagri (*for* fagrri)	
Gen.		fagrs	fagrar (*for* fagrrar)	
Plur. Nom.	fögr'	fagrir	fagrar	
Acc.	fögr'	fagra	fagrar	
Dat.		fögrum		
Gen.		fagra (for fagrra)		

Definite Form.

Nom.	fagra	fagri	fagra
Acc.	fagra;	fagra;	fögru.

92. Words whose characteristic letter (Kjendebogstav) is *l* after a double vowel, or, if dissyllabic, stands after any vowel, change it in the termination of *r* into *ll* (39) as:

heilt, heill, heil and in f. g. *Dat.* heilli, *Gen.* heillar, *Plur. Gen.* heilla;
gamalt, gamall, gömul, *Dat.* gamalli, *Gen.* gamallar *Plur. Gen.* gamalla; thus also:
þagalt *or* þögult, þögull, þögul etc.
Before terminations, beginning with a vowel, contractions occur as: gamlan, gamla, gömlu, gömlum. *Def. Form.* gamla,

gamli etc., but: heimilt or heimult does not contract. Fölt, fölr, föl, does not contract its *lr* into *ll*, being a monosyllable with a simple vowel.

93. In two words the *l* is dropped in the neuter before the characteristic letters *t*, *ð*, except in a different declension in the m. g. Acc.; it is declined

lítið, lítill, lítil, *Acc.* m. g. lítinn (for lítiln) f. g. litla, *Dat.* litlu, litlum, lítilli etc.

It will be observed that the vowel loses its accent, as soon as a concussion of consonants occurs. Writing lítið for lítit is for euphony's sake, and occurs in the best manuscripts; viz: the changing of this *t* into *ð*, as soon as the word receives *t* in the beginning, therefore ritað, but bakat etc. The second word is mikit, mikill, mikil, *Acc.* mikit, mikinn, mikla, *Dat.* miklu etc.

94. Those whose characteristic letter is *n* after a diphthong, or dissyllables, followed by a vowel, contract the *n* with *r* into *nn* (39) as:

vænt, vænn, væn, *Acc.* vænt, vænan, væna; *Dat.* vænu, vænum, vænni and in f. g. *Gen.* vænnar, *Plur.* *Gen.* vænna.

Dissyllables deviate besides in m. g. *Acc.* by contraction if the termination begins with a vowel, as:

Singular	*Nom.*	heiðit	heiðinn	heiðin
	Acc.	heiðit	heiðinn	heiðna
	Dat.	heiðnu	heiðnum	heiðinni
	Gen.	heiðins		heiðinnar
Plural	*Nom.*	heiðin	heiðnir	heiðnar
	Acc.	heiðin	heiðna	heiðnar
	Dat.		heiðnum	
	Gen.		heiðinna	
Def. Form	*Nom.*	heiðna;	heiðni;	heiðna etc.

95. In this manner are declined all regular participles of the closed Order of Verbs (which remain monosyllabic in the Dat.) as: ráðit, ráðinn, raðin; gefit, gefinn, gefin; tekit, tekinn, tekin etc.; also several of the 3rd order of the first chief Class (with modification of vowel) barit, barinn, barin. But these terminations stand in reality for -it, -iðr, ið a change of pronunciation in accordance with the

oldest danish language; they shorten the radical letter so
that *i* is dropped and ð is hardened into *d* or *t*, in words the
characteristic letter of which is a hard consonant as:

bart, barðr̃, börð; tamt, tamdr̃, tömd; vakt,
vaktr̃, vökt.

In this manner we find in some of these words a double
or triple form, of which the contracted one is the oldest;
those in *it*, *inn*, *in*, are modern Icelandic. — The words of
double form receive the general mixed declension after the
euphony, as:

Sing.	*Nom.*	vakit (*wakened*)	vakinn	vakin
	Acc.	vakit	vakinn	vakta
	Dat.	vöktu	vöktum	vakinni
	Gen.	vakins		vakinnar
Plural	*Nom.*	vakin	vaktir	vaktar
	Acc.	vakin	vakta	vaktar
	Dat.		vöktum	
	Gen.		vakinna·	
Def. Form.	*Nom.*	vakta	vakti	vakta etc.

As a proof of the real use of contractions by the ancients,
we cite:

kraft (Fms. 4,122 and 176), þaktr (Fms. 2,305); but,
þakiðr, (Grimnism. 9), dult (Islándíngas. 2,243);
huldr (Snorra-Edda 136), skilt (Fms. 6,220).

The modern forms are:

krafit, þakinn, dulit, hulinn·, skilit.

96. There is another kind of words which contracts as:
auðigt, rig-t, *Plur.* auðug, auðgir, auðgar;
málugr̃, málgir; öflugr̃, öflgir etc., but it is rare and
not irregular. Heilagt, -lagr̃, -lög contracts in the shortened forms *ei* into *e*, *Plur.* heilög, helgir, helgar, *def.*
Form helga, helgi, helga. The root *ill* is accented in the
n. g. íllt, illr̃, ill·, and *sann* contracts *nn* with *t* into *tt*:
satt, sannr̃, sönn; allt, allr̃, öll wants the def. form,
because it is definite in itself.

97. Compound Adjectives in *a* are not declinable as:
einskipa (Fms. 7,123), sundrskila (Fms. 11,131). But
there are some, in which the gender is shown in the Nom.
in the m. g. in -*i*, f. g. in -*a* as: sammœðri (Fms. 6,50),

sammœðra, forvitri, forvitra (Fms. 6,56) also: örviti (Fms. 7,158), málóði (Færeyjíngas S. 218), fulltiði (Egilss. 185).

The Comparison of Adjectives.

98. *The Comparative* is formed in Icelandic by: *–ara* (neut.), *ari* (masc.), *ari* (fem.), (kalda-ra, *colder;* harða-ra, *harder*); which takes the place of the *a* in the definite form. The fem. Sing. and all genders of the Plur. retain *i* everywhere (rarely Dat. in *–um*) as: spaka, Comparative; spakara

	Neut.	Masc.	Fem.
Sing. Nom.	spakara	spakari	spakari
Gen. Dat. Acc.	spakara	spakara	spakari
Plur. Nom. Gen. Dat. Acc.		spakari	

99. *The Superlative* is formed by adding to the root *–ast, astr, ust*, and is thus declined:

		Neut.	Masc.	Fem.
Indef. form.	*Nom.*	spakast	spakastr	spökust
	Acc.	spakast	spakastan	spakasta etc.
Def. form.	*Nom.*	spakasta	spakasti	spakasta
	Acc.	spakasta	spakasta	spökustu etc.

Those which shorten in the Posit., also do so in the other degrees, if the same cause exists, namely, that the termination begins with a vowel, as:

auðgara, auðgari, auðgast, auðgastr, auðgust etc.

100. There is however in many cases a shorter manner of formation for these degrees, namely by dropping the final *–a* and adding for the Comparative *–ra, –ri, –ri*, and for the Superlative *–st, –str, –st*. The modification of vowels which requires *–r* takes place (see 33. 34).

hit fagra	fegra	-ri fegrst	fegrstr	fegrst
— lága	lægra	-ri lægst	lægstr	lægst, *lowest*
— lánga	leingra	-ri leingst	leingstr	leingst, *longest*
or langa	lengra	-ri lengst	lengstr	lengst
hit þraungva	þreingra	-ri þreingst -str		-st, *closest*
or þröngva	þrengra	-ri þrengst -str		-st, *narrowest*
hit stóra	stœrra	-ri stœrst -str		-st, *greatest*

hit únga	ýngra	-ri	ýngst	-stŕ	-st, *youngest*
— þunna	þynnra	-ri	þynnst	-stŕ	-st, *thinnest*
— djúpa	dýpra	-ri	dýpst	-stŕ	-st, *deepest*
— dýra	dýrra	-ri	dýrst	-stŕ	-st, *dearest*
— væna;	vænna	-ri;	vænst	-stŕ	-st, *prettiest.*

The word mjótt, mjór, mjó, *small,* hit mjófa does not modify the vowel, although it takes the shorter termination mjórra, mjóst.

101. Some form their degrees in both manners, thus we meet with:

djúpara, djúpari, djupast, -astŕ, -ust

the shorter form almost always belongs to the old language.

Several take the shorter form in the Comparative and the longer one in the Superlative, as:

seint, seinna, seinast,
sælt, sælla, sællast;
nýtt, nýrra, nýjast.

102. The following are quite irregular:

Positive.		*Comp.*	*Superl.*
góða, gott,	hit góða	betra	bezt-a *best*
íllt	— illa		
vánt	— vánda	verra	verst-a *worst*
mikit	— mikla	meira	mest-a *greatest*
lítið	— litla	minna	minnst-a *least*
mart (margŕ, mörg)		fleira	flest *) *most*
gamalt; — gamla;		ellra	ellst-a *eldest;*
		eldra;	elzt-a:

103. Some compar. and superl. are formed from adverbs, prepos. and subst. and have therefore no positive, as:

(norðŕ)	nyrðra	norðast, nyrðst,	*northmost*
(austŕ)	eystra	austast	*eastmost*
(suðŕ)	syðra	syðst (synnst)	*southmost*
(vestŕ)	vestra	vestast	*westmost*
(fram)	fremra	fremst	*foremost*
(aptŕ)	eptra	aptast, epzt	*aftermost*
(út)	ytra	yzt	*outmost*
(inn)	innra	innst	*inmost*

---

*) This is not used definitely except in the plural: hin mörgu, hinir fleiri, hinar flestu mostly used by the moderns.

(of)	efra	efst	*highest*
(niðr̂)	neðra	neðst	*nethermost*
(for)	fyrra	fyrst	*first*
(síð)	síðara	síðast	*latest*
(heldr̂)	heldra	helzt	*ratherest*
(áðr̂)	æðra	æðst	*erst*
(fjarri)	(firr)	first	*farthest*
(ná-)	(nær, nærr)	næst	*nearest*

Fremra and síðara, have a regular positive, with different significations:

framt, framr̂, frðm, *excellent, valiant* (poetically); sítt, síðr̂, síð, *shallow, flat.*

104. Adjectives which have no positive, receive no comparisons, as allt (96) and those ending in -*i*, or -*a* (97) as well as the Pres. part. pass. in -*andi*. But these words can yet be increased or decreased by means of the adverbs:

meir, mest, or heldr̂, helzt, or: minnr̂ (miðr̂), minnst (minzt), síðr̂, sízt.

III. Pronouns.

105. The first two personal pronouns have a dual, which is commonly used as the plural, whilst the old pl. only occurs in the high style.

Sing.	1. *Person*	2. *Person*	3. *Person*
Nom.	ek (eg)	þú	—
Acc.	mik (mig)	þik (þig)	sik (sig)
Dat.	mer	þer	ser
Gen.	mín	þín	sín

	Dual	*Plural*	*Dual*	*Plural*	*Plural*
Nom.	vit (við)	ver	þit	þer	—
Acc.	okkr̂	oss	ykkr̂	yðr	sik (sig)
Dat.	okkr̂	oss	ykkr̂	yðr̂	ser
Gen.	okkar	vár;	ykkar	yðvar	sín

The third person has neither Neuter nor Plural which are replaced by the defin. pron. þat, sá, sú, which is thus declined:

Nom.	hann	hon (hún)
Acc.	hann	hana
Dat.	hánum (em)	henni
Gen.	hans	hennar

106. From the Genitive of the personal pronoun, are formed seven possessive pronouns:

of the 1st person Sing. mitt minn mín (*mine*)
- - 2nd - - þitt þinn þín (*thine*)
- - 3rd - - sitt sinn sín (*his*)
- - 1st - Dual okkart okkarr okkur (*your*)
- - 2nd - - ykkart ykkarr ykkur
- - 1st - Plural várt várr vár
- - 2nd - - yðvart yðvarr yður

The three first are declined like the article (74), only they receive a double *t* in the Neutr. and an accent, when an *n* follows the *i*, as: míns, míns, minnar. The four last pronouns are declined like indefinite adjectives, but they only take *n* (instead of *an*) in the Acc. Masc. as: okkarn (not okkaran), várn (not váran) etc., but the dissyllabic ones contract as usual, Dat. okkru, okkrum, okkari.

107. The demonstrative Pronoun is irregular:
þat, sá, sú, *that*; þetta, þessi, þessi *this*;
hinn, hin, *that, the other*; declined thus:

Sing. Nom.	þat	sá	sú	þetta	þessi	þessi
Acc.	þat	þann	þá	þetta	þenna	þessa
Dat.	því	þeim	þeirri	þessu	þessum	þessi (-arri)
Gen.	þess	þess	þeirrar	þessa	þessa	þessar (-arrar)
Plur. Nom.	þau	þeir	þær	þessi	þessir	þessar
Acc.	þau	þá	þær;	þessi	þessa	þessar.

Dat. þeim þessum
Gen. þeirra þessarra.

and the article hit, hinn, hin (74) which very frequently drops the *h* and forms in it, inn, in, or even et, enn, en. These are all used as dem. pronouns, but the *t* is doubled in the n. g. as hitt, hinn, hin, nor is the *h* dropped or the *e* added, as its pronunciation sounds purer and more emphatic.

108. Relative and interrogative pronouns, are with the exception of er and sem, the same, as:
hvárt (hvort), hvárr, hvár, *which of the two*
hvert, hverr, hver, *which of many*
hvílíkt, *what like, of what kind*
both declined as the indef. Adjectiv; only that they take in the

Acc. m. g. -*n* instead of -*an;* and h v e r t inserts *j,* when the ending begins with the vowels *a* or *u,* as:

Acc. hvert, hvern, hverja;
Dat. hverju, hverjum, hverri.

The Skalds use in Acc. m. g. hverjan, *every one.*

Declension of *hvort* (*hvdrt*):

		Neut.	Masc.	Fem.	Neut.	Masc.	Fem.
Sing.	Nom.	hvort	hvorr	hvor	hvert	hverr	hver
	Acc.	hvort	hvorn	hvora	hvert	hverjan	hverja
	Dat.	hvoru	hvorum	hvorri	. hverju	hverjum	hverri
	Gen.	hvors	hvors	hvorrar	hvers	hvers	hverrar
Plur.	Nom.	hvor	hvorir	hvorar	hver	hverír	hverjar
	Acc.	hvor	hvora	hvorar	hver	hverja	hverjar
	Dat.	hvorum	hvorum	hvorum	hverjum	hverjum	hverjum
	Gen.	hvorra	hvorra	hvorra	hverra	hverra	hverra.

109. There is also in the old norsk language a separate form for the interrogative pronoun *what;* it is thus declined :

		Neuter g.	Common g.
Sing.	Nom.	hvat	hverr (hvarr)
	Acc.	hvat	hvern (hvarn)
	Dat.	hvi	hveim
	Gen.	hvess	hvess;

in common speech *hvat* is only used a as pron. and h v í, as an adjective.

110. The indefinite pronoun is partly primitive, partly derived from other interr. pron. Primitive is:

eitt, einn, ein, *one, each one, alone;* sometimes it is declined like v æ n t (94) except that *nt* in n. g. takes *tt,* and that the Acc. m. g. has a double form as:

einn and einan.

111. A n n a t (*aliud, alterum, secundum*) *the one, the second, another,*

has a very irregular declension, thus:

		N.	M.	F.
Sing.	Nom.	annat	annarr	önnur
	Acc.	annat	annan	aðra
	Dat.	öðru	öðrum	annarri
	Gen.	annars	annars	annarrar

Plur. Nom. önnur   aðrir   aðrar
    Acc. önnur   aðra   aðrar

Dat.   öðrum
Gen.   annarra

It has the same form when the article is added, hit annat, the other, second; but when the question is of two, no article is used.

112. Bæði, *both,* is only used in the Plural:

Nom.	bæði	báðir	báðar
Acc.	bæði	báða	báðar
Dat.	báðum	báðum	báðum
Gen.	beggja	beggja	beggja.

113. The most important of the derivatives are:
hvárttveggja, hvárrtveggi, hvártveggja, *each one of two;* both parts are declined: hvárt (like 108) and tveggja like an adj. in defin. form, therefore in Plural:

hvártveggju, hvárirtveggju, hvárartveggju etc.

Annathvárt, annarrhvárr, önnurhvár, *one of two, one part of many parts,* has also a double declension, particularly in the Sing.; in the newer language the last part is mixed with hvert, and is therefore generally met with an inserted *j,* as:

öðruhverju for öðruhváru etc.

We also find: [*other*
hvart (or hvat) annat, hvárr annan, hvár aðra, *each*
and hvert annat,   hverr annan, hver aðra
or in Plur. hvert önnur, hverr aðra,   hver aðrar
in this case it is not compounded.

Hvárigt, hvárigr hvárig (or hvárugt etc.), (*none of the two, no part of the other*) is declined like an adjective indefinite form.

Sitthvat, or sitthvárt, sinnhvárr, sínhvár (*each his own, each one's*) is used divided, but sitt stands first. More frequently is used:

sitthvert, sinnhverr etc. as: þeir líta sinn í vherja átt, *each looks to his own side.*

114. Without reference to two, is used:
eitthvat (Germ. *etwas*) some, or:
eitthvert, einnhverr, einhver.

115. Nokkut (danish *noget*) *any*, is contracted from
nak and hvert, hvat or hvart, in which *ve* or *va* is contracted into *u*; this has many forms, of which we give the
oldest and most correct one.

Sing.	*Nom.*	nakkvart	nakkvarr	nökkur or nokkor
	Acc.	nakkvart	nakkvarn	nakkvara or nokkora
	Dat.	nökkuru	nökkurum	nakkvarri
	Gen.	nakkvars		nakkvarrar
Plur.	*Nom.*	nökkur	nakkvarir	nakkvarar
	Acc.	nökkur	nakkvara	nakkvarar
	Dat.		nökkurum	
	Gen.		nakkvarra.	

In n. g. also nakkvat, if derived from hvat, Dat. nökkví
Sometimes nökkut, nökkurr, nökkur,
and often nokkut, nokkurr, nokkur,
which has been adopted in the modern language. The two
last forms are also abridged by the moderns as:

Dat. nokkru, nokkrum, nokkurri

116. The negative pronoun is a compound of eitt, einn,
ein and the negative termination -*gi*, -*ki*, which also takes
many irregular forms; the oldest and most correct seem to be:

Sing.	*Nom.*	ekki (for eitki)	eingi	eingi
	Acc.	ekki	eingan (eingi)	einga
	Dat.	eingu (einugi)	eingum	eingri
	Gen.	eingis, einkis,	einskis	eingrar
Plur.	*Nom.*	eingi	eingir	eingar
	Acc.	eingi	einga	eingar
	Dat.		eingum	
	Gen.		eingra	

The syllable eing is often found contracted into eng;
thus in the Acc.: engan, enga; and this *eng* changes with
öng, as: öngan, önga; or with an inserted *v*
as: öngvan, öngva,
Dat. öngu, öngum, öngri,
or even: öngarri, Gen. öngarrar, it also lengthens into
aung, as: aungan, aunga, or aungvan, aungva.
But in n. g. and m. g. Gen. occur the changes of *ei*,
or *i* in the chief syllable, not önkis, aunskis.

117. *Numerals.*

Cardinal Numbers.	Ordinal Numbers.
one eitt, einn, ein;	*the first* fyrsta, -i, -a;
two tvau (tvö), tveir, tvær;	– *second* annat, annarr, önnur;
three þrjú, þrír, þrjár;	– *third* þriðja, þriði, þriðja;
four fjögur, fjórir, fjórar;	4th fjórða, -i, -a;
five fimm;	5th fimta, -i, -a;
6 sex;	6th sètta, (sjötta);
7 sjau (sjö);	7th sjaunda, sjönda(sjöunda)
8 átta;	8th átta (áttunda);
9 níu;	9th níunda;
10 tíu;	10th tíunda;
11 ellifu;	11th ellifta;
12 tólf;	12th tólfta;
13 þrettán;	13th þrettánda;
14 fjórtán;	14th fjórtánda;
15 fimtán;	15th fimtánda;
16 sextán;	16th sextánda;
17 sautján (seytján);	17th sautjánda (seytjánda);
18 átján;	18th átjánda;
19 nítján;	19th nítjánda;
20 tuttugu;	20th tuttugasta;
21 tuttugu ok eitt etc.;	21st tuttugasta ok fyrsta etc.
30 þrjátíu;	30th þrítugasta;
40 fjörutíu;	40th fertugasta;
50 fimtíu;	50th fimtugasta;
60 sextíu;	60th sextugasta;
70 sjautiu (sjötíu);	70th sjautugasta (sjötugasta);
80 áttatíu;	80th áttatugasta;
90 níutíu;	90th nítugasta;
100 hundrað, tíutíu;	100th hundraðasta;
110 hundrað ok tíú, ellifutíu;	110th hundraðasta ok tíunda;
120 h. ok tuttugu, stórt hundrað;	120th h. ok tuttugasta;
200 tvau hundrað etc.	200th tvau hundraðasta;
1000 þúsund	1000th þúsundasta

118. The four first of the numeral pron. are declined. Eitt (see 110,) the others in the Plural thus:

Plural Nom.	tvau	tveir	tvær	þrjú	þrír	þrjár
Acc.	tvau	tvá	tvær	þjrú	þrjá	þrjár
Dat.		tveim (tveimr)			þrim (þrimr)	
Gen.		tveggja.			þriggja.	

Plural Nom.	fjögur	fjórir	fjórar
Acc.	fjögur	fjóra	fjórar
Dat.	·	fjórum	
Gen.		fjögurra	

119. Those compounded with -*tíu*, have often another form in -*tigir*, -*tigi* as: þrjátigir, þrjátigi, but are not further declined, as: þrjátigi ok fimm árum — Landn. pag. 2, still more visible in the noun tigr̃ (tugr', togr̃, tögr̃), *Plur.* tigir, as: sex tigir, Sverriss. pag. 230 and átta tigir, Hk. 3,357. — Hundraд is a regular noun (55). The ancients almost always reckoned by the *great hundred* (120) so that hálft hundraд counted for 60 etc. Púsund (þúshundraд) is irregular (62).

120. From the ordinal Numbers are formed, those ending in   -*tugt, -tugr, -tug* (-*togt* or *tögt*),
and   -*rætt, -rœдr, -rœд*, as:

the 2nd part: tvítugt, tugr, tug; the 8th part: áttrœtt, -rœдr̃, -rœд;
- 3rd -   þrítugt;   - 9th -   nírœtt,
- 4th -   fertugt;   - 10th -   tírœtt;
- 5th -   fimtugt;   - 11th -   ellifurœtt;
- 6th -   sextugt;   - 12th -   ólfrœtt.
- 7th -   sjautugt (sjötugt);

The half is expressed by: hálft, hálfr̃, hálf, as: hálf-þrítugt, halffertogr̃ etc. which points out that 5 has been deducted from the last ten, thus:
hálffertogr̃ = 35, hálfáttrœдr̃ = 75.

The Verb.

121. Verbs are divided like the substantives into two chief orders the 1st or *open*, with the vowel in its termination;
2nd or *closed*, with a consonant

The first has more than one syllable in the Imperfect, the second is monosyllabic.

The *open* order is subdivided into 3 classes:
1st Cl. has three syllables in the Imperfect, with vowel *a*,
2nd Cl. has two syllables in the Imperfect, with vowel *i*,
3rd Cl. has two syllables with change or modification of vowel

(it has in the 1st person *us*, but seems originally to have had
the vowel *u*).

The *closed* order has two manners of inflection.

1st Cl. the one in which the change of vowel takes place
in the Indicative and Conjunctive of the Imperfect; the Part.
takes the same vowel of the main syllable as the present tense.

2nd Cl. contains the modification of the vowel of the Imperfect in the Part. with some exceptions.

Each of these two conjugations is subdivided in three
classes according to the modification of the vowel of the Imperfect. There are therefore altogether 9 Conjugations in which
every regular and irregular verb is included.

122. The following table will show the distinctive feature
of each:

I. Open Order.

1st *Form.*

		Pres. Indic.	Imperfect.	Sup.
1st *Class*	ek	ætla	ætlaða	ætlat
2nd -	-	heyri	heyrða	heyrt
3rd -	-	spyr	spurða	spurt.

II. Closed Order.

2nd *Form.*

1st *Class*	ek	drep	drep	drap	drepit
2nd -	-	ræð	ráð	réð	raðit
3rd -	-	dreg	drag	dró	dregit.

3rd *Form.*

1st *Class*	ek	renn	rann	*Pl.* runnum	runnit
2nd -	-	lít	leit	- litum	litið
3rd -	-	byð	bauð	- buðum	boðit.

123. It must be borne in mind, that the Indicative and
Conjunctive distinguish the Present and Imperfect, the Imperative is only used in the Present.

The *Infinitive* and *Participle* are only single forms, but
they are both declined like nouns.

The *Supine* is the Participle in n. g.

The *Participles* end generally in *-st*, in the oldest language in *sk* (an abbreviation of *sik*).

124. **1ˢᵗ Open Order.**

· *1ˢᵗ Form.*

kalla, *to call;* brenna, *to burn;* telja, *to tell.*

		1ˢᵗ *Class.*	2ⁿᵈ *Class.*	3ʳᵈ *Class.*
Indicative		Active.		
Pres. Sing.	1.	ek kalla	brenni	tel
	2.	þú kallar	brennir	telr
	3.	hann kallar	brennir	telr
Plur.	1.	ver köllum	brennum	teljum
	2.	þer kallit	brennit	telit
	3.	þeir kalla	brenna	telja
Imp. Sing.	1.	ek kallaða (i)	brenda (i)	talda (i)
	2.	þú kallaðir	brendir	taldir
	3.	hann kallaði	brendi	taldi
Plur.	1.	ver kölluðum	brendum	töldum
	2.	þer kölluðut	brendut	töldut
	3.	þeir kölluðu	brendu	töldu
Conjunctive				
Pres. Sing.	1.	ek kalla (i)	brenna (i)	telja (teli)
	2.	þú kallir	brennir	telir
	3.	hann kalli	brenni	teli
Plur.	1.	ver kallim	brennim	telim
	2.	þer kallit	brennit	telit
	3.	þeir kalli	brenni	teli
Imp. Sing.	1.	ek kallaði (a)	brendi (a)	teldi (a)
	2.	þú kallaðir	brendir	teldir
	3.	hann kallaði	brendi	teldi
Plur.	1.	ver kallaðim	brendim	teldim
	2.	þer kallaðit	brendit	teldit
	3.	þeir kallaði	brendi	teldi
Imp. Sing.	2.	kalla (-ðu)	brenn (-du)	tel (-du)
Plur.	1.	köllum (ver)	brennum	teljum
	2.	kallit (þer)	brennit	telit
Infinitive		at kalla	brenna	telja
Part.		kallanda, i	brennanda, i	teljanda, i
Sup.		kallat.	brent.	talıt (talt).

		1ˢᵗ Class.	2ⁿᵈ Class.	3ʳᵈ Class.
Indicative		**Passive.**		
Pres. Sing.	1.	kallast	brennist	telst
	2.	kallast	brennist	telst
	3.	kallast	brennist	telst
Plur.	1.	kollumst	brennumst	teljumst
	2.	kallizt	brennizt	telizt
	3.	kallast.	brennast.	teljast.
Imp. Sing.	1.	kallaðist	brendist	taldist
	2.	kallaðist	brendist	taldist
	3.	kallaðist	brendist	taldist
Plur.	1.	kölluðumst	brendumst	töldumst
	2.	kölluðuzt	brenduzt	tölduzt
	3.	kölluðust.	brendust.	töldust.
Conjunctive				
Pres. Sing.	1.	kallist	brennist	telist
	2.	kallist	brennist	telist
	3.	kallist	brennist	telist
Plur.	1.	kallimst	brennimst	telimst
	2.	kallizt	brennizt	telizt
	3.	kallist.	brennist.	telist.
Imp. Sing.	1.	kallaðist	brendist	teldist
	2.	kallaðist	brendist	teldist
	3.	kallaðist	brendist	teldist
Plur.	1.	kallaðimst	brendimst	teldimst
	2.	kallaðizt	brendizt	teldizt
	3.	kallaðist.	brendist.	teldist.
Imp. Sing.	2.	kallast-u	brend-u	telst-u
Plur.	1.	köllumst (ver)	brennumst	teljumst
	2.	kallizt (þer).	brennizt.	telizt.
Infinitive		at kallast.	brennast.	teljast.
Part.		(kallandist).	(brennadist).	(teljamdist).
Sup. Pass.		kallazt.	brenzt	talizt (talzt).

125. Many of the personal terminations are unsettled, we have taken as the regular one those which have most claim to be called so. The 1ˢᵗ Person Pres. has sometimes *r*, and becomes alike to the 2ⁿᵈ and 3ʳᵈ Person, as:

ek kallar, ek brennir, ek telr,

but the frequent and best use, as well as contractions, show the *r* to be spurious as

kallag, brennig, telk, *for* kalla ek etc.,
hyggig, hykk *for* hygg ek etc.

126. It is more correct to end the 1ˢᵗ Pers. of the Imperfect in -*a*, than in -*i*, for the preceding part of the verb has always those vowels which harmonize with *a* and not with *i*, except when *i* in the Present has been substituted by derivation and runs in every tense through the entire word, as brenni, from brann.

127. The 1ˢᵗ Pers. of the Conj. Present is also more correctly ended in *a* than *i*, but both are frequently used, and good manuscripts prefer in certain cases the -*i*.

Abbreviations like hug ð ak (Lodbrkv. 24) munak (Snorra E. 35) also prove the termination -*a*.

The 1ˢᵗ Person Plural has -*im*, in harmony with the other termination, and by a general use of the ancients; in the modern language this person has been changed into -*um* as the Indicative (köllum, brennum, teljum).

128. The 1ˢᵗ Pers. of the Conj. Imp. has sometimes -*a* instead of *i* in ancient writers, chiefly used by the Skalds; but it is less correct considering the vowel of the chief syllable. It is therefore less correct to say vek þa ek than vekti ek
bæþa ek - bæði ek
(Snorra E. 97) except the third person be taken, which could perhaps be placed in the 1ˢᵗ pers., as is done in the oriental languages.

It is however always correct in the plural that the 1ˢᵗ pers. should terminate in -*im*, the 2ⁿᵈ in -*it*, although, -*um*, *ut*, is to be met with in more recent Mss. In all verbs, (except the 1ˢᵗ Class) with the modification of vowel in the principal syllable, which requires the termination -*i*, as:

köllu ð um, köllu ð ut, brendum, brendut, teldum, teldut.

The 3ʳᵈ Pers. is only found in *u*, in the modern icelandic of the northern dialect, as:

kolluðu, brendu, teldu

although these forms have crept into all Mss. The two first persons in -*um* and -*ut* are generally wrong, even if they appear in the Sagas or the Skalds.

129. It must be observed that the Imperative 1st and 2nd person harmonize with the Indicative Present. The third person is formed by the Conjunctive, as: Nj. 67:

> köllum karl enn skegglausa!

and Sverriss. S. 185:

> Týnom Birkibeinum!
> beri Sverrir hlut verra! etc.

130. In reflective verbs the 1st Person Plur. -umst, is often seen, also in the 1st Pers. Sing. as:

> eigi berjumst ek (Fms. 6, 25),
> ek hugðumst (Snorra E. 97).

131. The terminations of the Plural drop in the 1st Pers. -m, in the 2nd Pers. -t (ð) if immediately followed by a pronoun, particularly in the Imperative, as:

> megu ver, megu þit (Nj. 17),
> föru ver! fari her!

132. The 1st Class is very regular. Words which have no -a in the principal syllable take naturally no modification, as:

> ek skipa, ver skipum, ek skipaða, ver skipuðum,

not even those which have ö, change it into a, although the -u termin., which seems to have .occasioned the ö in the principal syllable, is dropped and terminates in -a, as:

> ek fjötra, ver fjötrum, ek fjötraða, ver fjötruðum,
> fjötrat.

133. The other class has some irregularities, occasioned by the vowel -i in the Imperfect and Part., which is dropped if the consonant is the same as the root. The ancients make it single, where it was double as:

byggi	bygða	bygt	-gðr	-gð
hnýkki	hnykta	hnykt	-ktr	-kt
kippi	kipta	kipt	-ptr	-pt
kenni	kenda	kent	-dr	-d
stemmi	stemda	stemt	-dr	-d
hvessi	hvesta	hvest	-tr	-t.

134. The termination is still more influenced by the consonant of the root

-ta after p, t, k, s,

-da after *b*, *ð* (changed into *d*) *fl, gl, fn, gn, m,*
-ða after *f, g, r* and every vowel; with another consonant
preceding *t* is dropped behind *tt* or *t*,
-d behind *nd* etc., *ð* behind *rð*, as:

steypi	steypta	steypt	-ptr	-pt
veiti	veitta	veitt	-ttr	-tt
krœki	krœkta	krœkt	-ktr	-kt
læsi	læsta	læst	-str	-st
kembi	kembda	kembt	-bdr	-bd
reiði	reidda	reidt	-ddr	-dd
efli	eflda	eflt	-ldr	-ld
nefni	nefnda	nefnt	-ndr	-nd
flæmi	flæmda	flæmt	-mdr	-md
deyfi	deyfða	deyft	-fðr	-fð
vígi	vígða	vígt	-gðr	-gð
læri	lærða	lært	-rðr	rð
þjai	þjaða	það	-ðr	-ð
hitti	hitta	hitt	-ttr	-tt
vænti	vænta	vænt	-tr	-t
heimti	heimta	heimt	-tr	-t
sendi	senda	sent	-dr	-d
virði	virða	virt	-ðr	-ð.

135. Those in *-lg*, *-ng*, receive in some Mss. *-lgða*, *-ngða*;
in others *-lgda*, *-ngda*; as fylgda, tengda (Fms. 7) —
Those in *l*, *n* receive partly *-da*, partly *-ta*, as: fell, fellda
(felda); mæli, mælta, sýni, sýnda; ræni, rænta.

136. Those whose last consonant is *g* or *k*, even with
another consonant preceding, do not always drop the *i*, but
change it into *j*, which they retain before the terminations *-a*
and *-u*, as:

byggi, ver byggjum, þeir byggja, at byggja,
byggjanda; likewise:

ek fylgi, ver fylgjum; ek syrgi, ver syrgjum;

ek teingi, ver teingjum; ek fylki, ver fylkjum;
ek merki, ver merkjum.

137. It will be observed that this class does not modify
the vowel, having already received the modification in the first
person (-*i*), which is transmitted without regard to the termination. In some words this is not accidental; it seems as if

the characteristic letter should be *e*; these words have other irregularities, the most important of them are:

dugi	at duga	dugdka	*Conj.* dygði	dugat	
vaki	- vaka	vakta	- vekti	vakit -inn -in	
kaupi	- kaupa	keypta	- keypti	keipt -tr -t	
þoli	- þola	þolda	- þyldi	þolat	
þori	- þora	þorða	- þyrði	þorat	
uni	- una	unda	- yndi	unat	
vari	-. vara	varða	*or* varaða-i	varat	
trúi	- trúa	trúða	*Conj.* tryði	trúat	
næ	- ná	náða	- næði	nað	
lè (ljæ)	- lja	lèða	- lèði	lèð.	

138. To this class belongs the auxilliary verb „hefi" to have:

Indicative.				*Conjunctive.*			
Present.	*Sing.*	1.	hefi	*Present.*	*Sing.*	1.	hafa
		2. 3.	hefir			2.	hafir
	Plur.	1.	höfum			3.	hafi
		2.	hafit		*Plur.*	1.	hafim
		3.	hafa			2.	hafit
Imperf.	*Sing.*	1.	hafða			3.	hafi
		2.	hafðir	*Imperf.*	*Sing.*	1.	hefði
		3.	hafði			2.	hefðir
	Plur.	1.	höfðum			3.	hefði
		2.	höfðut		*Plur.*	1.	hefðim
		3.	höfðu.			2.	hefðit
						3.	hefði.
Imperat.	*Sing.*	2.	haf-ðu	*Infinit.* at hafa			
	Plur.	1.	höfum	*Part.* hafanda, i			
		2.	hafið	*Sup.* haft, -för, höfð.			

139. Sometimes the modification of a vowel appears in the Present:

	Sing.	1.	vaki	næ	veld
		2. 3.	vakir	nær	veldr
	Plur.	1.	vökum	nám (for náum)	völdum
		2.	vakit	náit	valdit
		3.	vaka;	na (for náa);	valda.

Veld is one of the most irregular verbs: *Imperf.* olli, *Conj.* ylli, *Sup.* valdit, now ollat, *Infin.* valda (only olla). In the Supine differs: lifi, lifði, lifat.

140. The third Class is monosyllabic in the Present Sing., but takes a -*j* before the finals in -*a*, -*u*. In the Imperfect it has like the preceding -*ta*, -*da*, or ð*a*, but more regularly *da* after *l*, *n*. In the Part. Past. it has sometimes the shortened sometimes the mixed form (95). The Imperfect and Part. Past. has only a double modification of vowel, either *e* into *a*, or *y* into *u*, as:

glep	at glepja	glapta	glepti	glapit (glapt),	*to lead astray*
let	- letja	latta	letti	latt,	*to let*
vek	- vekja	vakti	vekti	vakit,	*to waken*
kveð	- kvedja	kvaddi	kveddi	kvadt,	*to take leave*
vel	- velja	valda	veldi	valit,	*to chose*
ven	- venja	vanda	vendi	vanit,	*to wean*
tem	- temja	tamda	temdi	tamit,	*to tame*
kref	- krefja	krafða	krefði	krafit (kraft),	*to crave*
legg	- leggja	laggða	legði	(lagit) lagt,	*to lay down*
ber	- berja	barða	berði	barit (bart),	*to smite*
flyt	- flytja	flutta	flytti	flutt,	*to carry*
lyk	- lykja	lukta	lykti	lukt,	*to shut to*
þys	- þysja	þusta	þysti	þust,	*to rush on*
ryð	- ryðja	rudda	ryddi	rudt,	*to root out*
hyl	- hylja	hulda	hyldi	(hult) hulit,	*to hide*
styn	- stynja	stunda	styndi	(stunt) stunit,	*to groan*
rym	- rymja	rumda	rymdi	rumt,	*to roar*
tygg	- tyggja	tugða	tygði	tuggit,	*to chew*
spyr	- spyrja	spurða	spyrði	spurt,	*to ask*
lý	- lýja	lúða	lyði	lúit (lúð),	*to hammer.*

141. Irregular in the Sup. is: hygg, hugða, hugat. The five following do not change the vowel:

set	at setja	setta	setti	sett,	*to set*
sel	- selja	selda	seldi	selt,	*to sell*
skil	- skilja	skilda	skildi	(skilt) skilit,	*to separate*
vil	- vilja	vilda	vildi	viljat,	*to will*
flý	- flýja	flýða	flýði	flýit,	*to fly.*

of these vil is found in the ancient Manuscripts in the 2nd and 3rd person: vill (for vilr) sometimes to the 2nd person villtu or vilt, modific. form Infin. vildu for vilja.

The five following have in the Present:

segi	at segja	sagða	segði	sagt,	*to say*
þegi	- þegja	þagða	þegði	þagat,	*to be silent*
þykki	- þykkja	þótta	þœtti	þott,	*to think*
yrki	- yrkja	{ orta	yrti	ort	*to write verse*
		{ yrkta	yrkti	yrkt	*to work*
sœki	- sœkja	sótta	sœtti	sótt,	*to seek.*

142. Some are also irregular in the Present, where they become monosyll.; and like the Imperfect of the closed order, they are:

ann	at unna	unna	ynni	unt,	*to grant*
man	- muna	munda	myndi	munat,	*to remember*
kann	- kunna	kunna	kynni	kunnat,	*to be able*
man	- mundu }	munda	{ myndi	*wanting*	*will, would*
mun	- munu }		{ mundi		
skal	{ - skyldu }	skylda	skyldi	*wanting*	*shall, ought*
	{ - skulu }				
þarf	- þurfa	þurfta	þyrfti	þurft,	*to be needful*
á	- eiga	átta	ætti	átt,	*to own*
má	- mega	mátta	mætti	mátt, }	*to be able*
kná	- knega	knátta	knætti	(knátt), }	
veit	- vita	vissa	vissi	vitað,	*to know.*

A regular word unni, unta, ynti, unt must be distinguished from ann. For kná is also found knai, knáða, knàð.

143. The irregularities in the Present consist in these verbs, that the 1st and 3rd person are alike, the 2nd receives the termination -t or -st in words in which the principal letter is t, chiefly in the word veit; the 2nd pers. Plur. receives in some words -ut or -it, the 3rd pers. Plur. often receives -u (o) by the ancient, and -a by the modern writers, as:

Sing.	1. 3.	kann	skal	á	veit
	2.	kant	skalt	átt	veizt
Plur.	1.	kunnum	skulum	eigum	vitum
	2.	kunnit	skulut	eigut (i)	vitið (að)
	3.	kunna.	skulu.	eigu (a).	vita (u).

144.   IInd Closed Order.

IInd Form.

gefa, *to give*; láta, *to let*: fara, *to fare*.

		1st Class.	*2nd Class.*	*3rd Class.*
Indicative			Active.	
Pres. Sing.	1.	gef	læt	fer
2.	3.	gefr	lætr	ferr
Plur.	1.	gefum	látum	förum
	2.	gefit	látið	farit
	3.	gefa	láta	fara
Imp. Sing.	1.	gaf	lèt	fór
	2.	gaft	lèzt	fórt
	3.	gaf	lèt	fór
Plur.	1.	gáfum	lètum	fórum
	2.	gáfut	lètuð	fórut
	3.	gáfu.	lètu.	fóru.
Conjunctive				
Pres. Sing.	1.	gefa (i)	láta (i)	fara (i)
	2.	gefir	látir	farir
	3.	gefi	láti	fari
Plur.	1.	gefim	látim	farim
	2.	gefit	látið	farit
	3.	gefi	láti	fari
Imp. Sing.	1.	gæfi (a)	lèti (a)	fœri (a)
	2.	gæfir	lètir	fœrir
	3.	gæfi	lèti	fœri
Plur.	1.	gæfim	lètim	fœrim
	2.	gæfit	lètið	fœrit
	3.	gæfi	lèti	fœri
Imp. Sing.	2.	gef (-ðu)	lát	far
Plur.	1.	gefum	látum	förum
	2.	gefit	látið	farit
Inf.		at gefa	lata	fara
Part.		gefanda, i.	látanda, i.	faranda, i.
Sup.		gefit.	látið.	farit.

IIIrd Form.

brenna, *to burn*; grípa, *to gripe*; skjóta.

	1st Class.	2nd Class.	3rd Class.

Indicative   Passive.

			1st Class.	2nd Class.	3rd Class.
Pres.	Sing.	1.	brenn	gríp	skýt
	2. 3.		brennr	grípr	skýtr
	Plur.	1.	brennum	grípum	skjótum
		2.	brennit	grípit	skjótið
		3.	þrenna	gripa	skjóta
Imp.	Sing.	1.	brann	greip	skaut
		2.	brant	greipt	skauzt
		3.	brann	greip	skaut
	Plur.	1.	brunnum	gripum	skutum
		2.	brunnut	griput	skutuð
		3.	brunnu.	gripu.	skutu.
Conjunctive					
Pres.	Sing.	1.	brenna (i)	grípa	skjóta (i)
		2.	brennir	gripir	skjótir
		3.	brenni	grípi	skjóti
	Plur.	1.	brennim	grípim	skjótim
		2.	brennit	grípit	skjótið
		3.	brenni	grípi	skjóti
Imp.	Sing.	1.	brynni (a)	gripi (a)	skyti (a)
		2.	brynnir	gripir	skytir
		3.	brynni	gripi	skyti
	Plur.	1.	brynnim	gripim	skytim
		2.	brynnit	gripit	skytið
		3.	brynni	gripi	skyti
Imp.	Sing.	2.	brenn	gríp	skjót
	Plur.	1.	brennum	grípum	skjótum
		2.	brennit	grípit	skjótið
	Inf.		at brenna	grípa	skjóta
	Part.		brennanda, i	grípanda, i	skjótanda, i
	Sup.		brunnit.	gripit.	skotit.

145. As a singularity in the Conjugation of this closed Order, it must be noticed that those whose principal letter is- *s*,

take in the 2nd and 3rd person not *-r*, but in the 2nd *-t*, and retain in the 3rd the termination of the first, as:

ek les, þú lest, hann les, *Imp.* las, *Sup.* lesit;
ek blæs, þu blæst, hann blæs, *Imp.* blès; *Sup.* blásit;
ek rís, þú ríst, hann rís, *Imp.* reis, *Sup.* risit;
ek frýs, þú fryst, hann frýs, *Imp.* fraus, *Sup.* frosit.

No doubt this belongs to the modern icelandic language, not to the genuine old Norsk, in which the termination was without doubt *r*, contracted with *s* into *ss*:

ek eys, þú eiss (Lokagl. 4), hann eiss, ver ausum, *Imp.* jós, *Sup.* ausit. Also:
ek vex, þú vex (not þu *vext*), Snorra E. 114, hann vex, sst. ver vöxum, *Imp.* vóx or óx, *Sup.* vaxit.

The modern language applies this rule generally to those words, whose principal letter is *r* as:

eg fer, þú ferð, hann fer, for
ek fer, þú ferr, hann ferr,

which is generally the rule in the ancient language.

146. The 2nd form, 1st Class, contains some irregular verbs, as:

ek tred	at troða	trað	tráðum	træði	troðit,	*to tread*
- kem	- koma	kvam	kvámum	kvæmi	komit	*to come*
- sef	- sofa	svaf	sváfum	svæfi	sofit,	*to sleep*
- get	- geta	gat	gátum	gæti	getið,	*to beget*
- get	- geta	gat	gátum	gæti	getað,	*to talk of*
- et	- eta	at	-um	æti	etið,	*to eat*
- veg	- vega	vá	-gum	vægi	vegit,	*to kill*
- ligg	- liggja	lá	-gum	lægi	legit,	*to lie*
- þigg	- þiggja	þá	-gum	þægi	þegit,	*to receive*
- se	- sja	sá	-m	sæi	sèd (sèð),	*to see.*

For kvam etc. we find often kom-um, kæmi, rarely in the Imp. Sing. vág, lág, þág; the second person is þú vátt (Nj. 203), not *vágt*. The word se shortens, when *u* follows after *a*, as: in the Pres. sjám (ver), Hk. 1, 163, and in the Imperf. sáð (þer), Nj. 8. Part. Pass. adds *j* before *e* or takes the accent, as: in n. g. sèt (or sèð), in m. g. sènn (Fms. 5, 249) or séðr, in f. g. sèn.

147. To this class belongs also the auxiliary verb, ek em, *I am*:

		Indicative:	*Conjunctive:*	*Imperative:*
Pres.	*Sing.*	ek em (er) *I am.*	se	veri
		þú ert	ser	ver-tu (verir)
		hann er	se	veri
	Plur.	ver erum	sem	verum
		þer erut	seð	verit
		þeir eru.	se.	veri.
Imp.	*Sing.*	ek var *I was.*	væri (a)	*Infinitive:*
		þú vart	værir	*Pres.* at vera
		hann var	væri	*Part.* veranda, i
	Plur.	ver várum	værim	*Sup.* verit
		þer várut	værit	
		þeir váru	væri.	

148. Some have irregular modification of the vowels in
the Supine, as:

nem	at nema	nam	námum	næmi	numit
bregð	- bregða	brá	brugðum	brygði	brugðit
ber	- bera	bar	bárum	bæri	borit
sker	- skera	skar	skárum	skæri	skorit
stel	- stela	stal	stálum	stæli	stolit
fel	- fela	{ fal (fól	fálum fólum)	fæli	falit fólgit }

149. The second class has but few irregularities, these are:

heit	at heita	hèt -um -i		heitið
heiti	- heita	hèt -um -i		heitið
hángi	- hanga	hèkk	hengum -i	hángit
geing	- gánga	gèkk	gengum -i	gengit
fæ	- fá	fèkk	fengum -i	fengit.

150. Several belonging to this class are quite irregular in
the Imperfect:

ný	núa	nera -rum -ri	núit
sný	snúa	snera (Nj. 95) -rum -ri	snúit
rœ	róa	rera -rum -ri	róit
grœ	gróa	grera -rum -ri	gróit

they are conjugated according to the first form, namely 2nd pers.:
nerir, 3rd neri etc. In the old language we often find ð
or *ey* for *e*, in the new language *è*, as: nèra or nèri, snèri,
etc. The word ræð, which is regular in the old language,
forms in the new the Imperfect with additional *i*, rèði.

• 151. The third Class has the following irregularities:

svær	sverja	{ svarði	svörðum	sverði }	svarit,	to swear
		sór	sórum	sœri		
stend	standa	stoð	-um	stœði	staðit,	to stand
slæ	slá	sló	-gum	slœgi	slegit,	to strike
flæ	flá	fló	-gum	flœgi	flegit,	to flay
hlæ	hlæja	hló	-gum	hlœgi	hlegit,	to laugh
dey	deyja	dó	-gum	dœgi	dáit,	to die
spý	spýja	spjó	-m	—	spúit,	to spit.

In the Sing. Imperf. we find, although rarely

slóg, flóg, lóg, dóg.

The *g* is more frequently dropped in the Plur. of the Conj. Imperfect, as:

slóum, dón, hlœi (Fms. 2, 152).

152. Some verbs are quite irregular in the plural of the Imperfect, Indicative and Conjunctive, as:

vex	vaxa	óx	uxum	yxi	vaxit,	to wax, grow
eyk	auka	jók	jukum	jyki	aukit,	to increase
eys	ausa	jós	jusum	jysi	ausit,	to sprinkle
hleyp	hlaupa	hljóp	hlupum	hlypi	hlaupit,	to run, urge
bý	búa	bjó	bjuggum	bjyggi	búit,	to dwell
högg	höggva	hjó	hjuggum	hjyggi	höggvit,	to hew.

We also find óxum, hljópum, but this form is spurious, as the Conjunct. œxi, hljœpi is not used, but only yxi, hlypi, which presupposes in the plur. of the Indicat. uxum, hlupum.

153. The 1ˢᵗ form of the 3ʳᵈ Class has also the following irregular verbs:

finn	finna	fann	fundum •	fyndi	fundit,	to find
bind	binda	batt	bundum	byndi	bundit	to bind
vind	vinda	vatt	undum	yndi	undit	to wind
stíng	stínga	stakk	stúngum	stýngi	stúngit	to sting
spríng	springa	sprakk	sprúngum	sprýngi	sprúngit,	to split
geld	gjalda	galt	guldum	gyldi	goldit,	to be worth, pay
skelf	skjálfa	skalf	skulfum	skylfi	skolfit,	to shake
hverf	hverfa	hvarf	hurfum	hyrfi	horfit,	to diminish.

The last are regular with the exception of the accent in skjàlfa, such is also the auxilliary verb:

ek verð, at verða, varð, urðum, yrði, orðit.

Most of the regular verbs have *o* in the first syllable of the Sup.; only those which have *n* after the vowel, receive *u*; also

drekk, drakk, drukkit

because *kk* stands here for *nk* or *ngk* (38).

154. The second class is very regular. But the Verbs in -*ig* have in the Imperfect not only -*eig*, but also the 2ⁿᵈ form of the 2ᵈ Class in *e*, with a dropped *g*, as:

stíg   stíga   { steig   stigum   stigi }   stigit.
                 { stè   (stèum   stèi) }

Likewise: vík, víkja, veik or vèk (Paradism. S. 218).

155. The third class is also very regular; only a few have *ö* in the Imperfect; occasioned by a double Consonant following it, which is pronounced hard. Some in -*ng* take in the first syllable of the Sup. after a vowel *u*. These ought to be added to those which take *ö* in the Imperfect; but the extension of all vowels before -*ng* (34) is the reason that they generally take -*au*, as:

sökk   sökkva   sökk   sukkum   sykki   sokkit,   *to sink*
stökk   stökkva   stökk   stukkum   stykki   stokkit,   *to leap.*
hrökk   hrökkva   hrökk   hrukkum   brykki   hrokkit,   *to move quickly*
{sýng   sýngja   saung súngum   sýngi   súngit,} *to sing.*
{syng   syngva   söng sungum   syngi   sungit,}

Thus also slýng, slaung (Helgakv. Hundb. I. V. 33); slungit, and þrýng, þraung, þrúngit, which are however antiquated poetical words.

Auxiliary Verbs.

156. These auxiliary verbs are used to supply the wanting tenses by periphrase; they are very simple in the Old Norsk, and were less frequently in use than in the Danish, otherwise they are about the same.

Future periphr. man (mun) and skal;
Future preterite. munda, skylda;
Perfect. hefi, em (er);
Pluperfect. hafða, var,

f. i. with the auxiliary verbs em and verð.

Icelandic Grammar.   4

Indicative

Fut. periph.	ek man vera	ek man verða
	- skal vera	- skal verða
Fut. preter.	- munda vera	- munða verða
	- skylda vera	- skylda verða
Perfect.	- hefi verit	- hefi orðit
Pluperfect.	- hafða verit	- em orðinn
		- hafða orðit
		- var orðinn.

Conjunctive

Fut. periph.	ek muna (i) vera	ek muna (i) verða
	- skula (i) vera	- skula (i) verða
Fut. preter.	- myndi (a) vera	- myndi (a) verða
	- skyldi (a) vera	- skyldi (a) verða
Perfect.	- hafa (i) verit	- hafa (i) orðit
		- se ordinn
Pluperfect.	- hefði (a) verit	- hefði (a) orðit
		- væri (a) orðinn

Derivative Forms

Ind. Fut. per.	(at) munda vera	(at) munda verða
	- skyldu vera	- skyldu verða
Perfect.	- hafa verit	- hafa orðit
		- vera orðinn
Part. Perf.	- hafanda verit.	- hafandi orðit
		- hafanði orðinn.

The Part. Perf. was rarely used.

157. Passive.

Indicative

Pres.	ek em (er) kallaðr	talinn etc.
Imp.	- var kallaðr	talinn
Future.	- man (verða) kallaðr	talinn
Fut. pret.	- munda (verða) kallaðr	talinn
Perf.	- hefi verit kallaðr	talinn
Pluperf.	- hafða verit kallaðr	talinn

Conjunctive

Pres.	ek se kallaðr	talinn
Imp.	- væri (a) kallaðr	talinn
Future.	- muna (i) [verða] kallaðr	talinn

Fut. pret.	- myndi (a) [verða] kallaðr	talinn
Perf.	- hafa (i) verit kallaðr	talinn
Pluperf.	- hefði (a) verit kallaðr	talinn

Derivative Forms

Ind. Fut. per.	at vera kallaðr	talinn
Perf.	- mundu [verða] kallaðr	talinn
Pluperf.	- hafa verit kallaðr	talinn

These periphrase forms are rarely used in the order we have given, they are partly separated, partly transposed by inserted words.
Skal is used in an obligatory and assured sense. After man or skal — verða or vera is frequently left out. Vera is used for the present time, which has begun, verða, for the future time, which is now beginning, man and skal for the future time, not yet begun.

158. The Passive form in -*st*, has also derivatives, as:

ek man kallast	teljast
- munda kallast	teljast
- hefi kallazt	talizt
- hafða kallazt	talizt etc.

V. Particles.

159. This class of words, generally not inflected, take a comparison, they form the Comparative in -*a*, the Superlative in -*ast*; some have shorter forms in -*r*, -*st*:

opt	optar	optast	*often*
títt	tíðar	tíðast	*closely*
víða	víðar	víðast	*widely*
norðr	norðar	norðast	*northerly*
skamt	skemr	skemst	*shortly*
leingi	leingr	leingst	*long ago.*

160. Some are irregular or imperfect:

vel	betr	bezt	*good*
illa	verr	verst	*bad*
mjök	meir	mest	*much*
lítt	minnr (miðr)	minnst	*little*
gjarna	heldr	helzt	*rather*
úti	utar	yzt	*without*

4*

inni	innar	innst	*within*
uppi	ofar (efra)	ofarst (efst)	*up*
niðri	neðar	neðst	*beneath.*

The n. g. of the adjective in the 1ˢᵗ and 2ⁿᵈ degree has often two forms with different significations as:

utar, *outside* (opposite the door, but visible),
ytra, *without* (out of sight),
leingr and skemr, *shorter, only of time,*
leingra and skemra, *shorter, only of place.*

The Formation of Words.

161. The formation of words, much resembles the Danish, but it is more lively, richer and more certain. We do not intend to enter here into a minute disquisition, but one of the chief sources of derivation deserves attention, it is the Imperfect of the 2ⁿᵈ Order. From the plural are derived:

162. A) Nouns, such as:

dráp, from drep, dráp, drápum;
nám from nem, nam, námum;
fengr from fæ, fèkk, fengum;
sœri from sver, sór;
hlœgi from hlæ, hlóg;
fundr from finn, fann, fundum;
sprúnga from spríng, sprakk, sprúngum;
hvarf from hverf, hvarf;
stig from stíg, steig, stigum;
bit from bít, beit, bitum;
saungr (söngr) from sýng, saung (söng).

Sometimes there is no difference at all, and the noun seems to be the genuine old Imperfect, as:

bragð from bregð, brá;
boð from býð, bauð;
skot from skýt, skaut.

The plural brugðum seems to be formed from bragð and not from brá; also stigum from stig, not from steig, bitum from bit, not from beit; buðum, Conj. form byði, from boð, not from bauð; skutum, Conj. form skyti, from sk ot, not from sk au t. Related languages show the same, as for instance the english

I bite, bit, I shoot, shot, with *a bit, a shot,* as nouns; such is also the german:

beisse, biss, schiesse, schoss and the nouns: *Biss, Schuss.*

Sometimes the German language lengthens the vowel as in

steige, stieg; biete, bot;

but even these lengthened Imperfects harmonize with the Old Norsk nouns:

stig, boð, not steig, bauð.

But transitions occur from

ei into *i*

au (ey) into *o (u)*

even in the old norsk formation of words, as:

veik-t — vik-na; baugr, beygi — bogi, bugr.

163. B) *Adjectives* which show in the Active as well as Passive that the extention of the verb is possible. These are so much more remarkable, as they have entirely disapeared in the modern language, as:

dræp-t, dræp-r, dræp, *what one may kill;*

næm-t, *to take easily, contagious,*

á-fengr, *which is easily received, goes into the head, intoxicates;*

al-geng-t, (german *gäng und gäbe) current, usual,* from geng, gekk, gengum;

fœr-t, *navigable,* from fer, fór;

upp-tœk-t, *takeable,* from tek, tók.

fleyg-t, (german *flügge) fledged,* from flýg, flaug;

neýt-t, *useful,* from nýt, naut etc.

164. C) *Verbs,* which instead of the unobjective take the active signification, or if the root were active they take the figurative signification as:

svæfi, *to fall asleep,* from sef, svaf, sváfum;

sæti, *to watch,* from sit, sat, sátum;

hængi, *to hang up,* from hangi, hekk, hengum;

felli, *to fell,* from fell, fell-um;

breyti, *to alter,* from brýt, braut;

neyti, *to eat* etc.

Syntax.

165. In the position of sentences the Old Norsk resembles the Danish, but the definite inflection to which the ancients paid great attention, gave them greater scope and freedom in the composition of the sentence. — The most remarkable difference of this kind is the custom of placing the verb, particularly the Imperfect, before the noun or pronoun, as:

kallaði Njall þetta lögvörn; —
varu í þessu þá margir höfðingjar; —
ok fèkst þat af;
gengu hvârirtveggju þá; —
ríða þeir nú heim.

166. The numeral pronouns up to 29 are always added to the noun as adjectives, whether declinable or not, as:

þrír íslenzkir menn; fimtán bœndr; tuttugu skip (HK. 3, 344),

but 30 and the higher decimals govern the word in the Acc. as:

þrjátigi skipa; sextigi heiðingja (Fms. 6, 61); tíutigi manna (Fms. 7, 303).

The reason of this is, that the last part of this compound is a noun (119) as with

hundrað as: þrjú hundruð nauta.

167. The Verbs frequently govern the Gen. as in other languages, often the Dat. and Acc. Some govern two cases, two Gen., two Dat. or Gen. and Dat., Dat. and Acc. etc.

One of these rules has such expansion that we must specify it; it is this: a number of verbs govern the Dative, showing that a thing changes place and position, without being changed in its own basis, as:

sný, vendi, fleygi, kasta, skýt, lyptì, dreifi, sái, stýri, ræð etc.

Some take the Gen. in a different signification, as:

hann skaut öru til mannsins; but:
skjóttu manninn þann hinn mikla.

All Verbs which express a use, assistance, injury, saying etc. govern the Dative, some of them take two Datives, as:

hann lofaði henni þvi; hon svaraði hânum þvi.

Prepositions.

168. The following govern the Accusative:

um (of), *over*   umfram, *before*

umhverfis, *round about*   framyfir, *over*

í gegnum, *through, by*   framundir, *against,*

also a great many combinations with u m, as:

út um, *out of, outside,*

inn um; yfir um, í hring um (*around in a ring*),

and those signifying a position, as:

fyrir norðan, fyrir sunnan, fyrir ofan, fyrir neðan, fyrir utan, fyrir innan, also fyrir handan ána.

169. The Dativ govern:

af, *of*   hjá, *by*

frá, *from*   ásamt, *together with*

ör, yr, ur, or, *out*   gagnvart, *above*

undan, *out of*   mót, á móti, í móti, *against,*

with some combinations, as:

út af, upp frá, fram or, á undan (*before*).

frambjá, *by, over;*

í gegn, *against;*

á hendr, *against, in opposition;*

til handa, *for, for the best;*

also: nær, nærri, fjarri, *near, yet.*

170. The Genitive govern:

til, *to*   millum, á milli, á meðal, *between*

an, on, *without*   í stað (hans), *instead of* (*his*)

utan, *out of*   sakir (fyrir sakir) ⎫

innan, *within*   sökum   ⎬ *by means of,*

auk, *without*   vegna   ⎭

and the composita with megin, as:

báðum megin, *on both sides,*

öðrum megin, hinum megin, *on each side,*

þessum megin, *on this side,*

öllum megin, *on all sides.*

171. The Accusative and Dative govern:

á, *on*   eptir, *behind*

í, *to, in*   fyrir, *for*

með, *with*   undir, *under*

við, *with, by, against*   yfir, *over,*

and a great number of combinations with short, local adverbs, as:

upp á, út i, fram með, í staðinn fyrir, inn undir,
út yfir etc.

172. The preposition *at* governs three cases:

1) the Accusative in the signification „*after*" (obsolete),

2) the Dative in the sign. „*to, towards*" used of things,
places, and time „at sumri", *towards summer*,

3) the Genitive in the signification „*at, in.*"

173. It often happens that a preposition is found before
a noun, without governing the same; in such a case the prep.
belongs to the verb; in reading a short stop is made between
prep. and noun. As:

> svá at þegar tók af höfuðit,
> *so that (it) straight took off the head.*

174. The preposition is often found behind the verb in
relative sentences, chiefly where the demonstr. pronoun is not
declined, as:

> Sverrir konúngr hafði viðsèt þessi snöru
> er þeir ætluðu hann í veiða.
> *The king Sverrir had seen the cord*
> *with which they thought to catch him.*

The prepos. -*i* is accented, but forms no composite with veiða,
as íveiða is no word.

Prosody.

175. The old verse of the Skalds may be reduced to three
Orders; corresponding to the three manners of rhyme in which
the chief poems of the old Icelandic tongue are written.

They are all divided into sing-verses or strophes (vísa,
staka) which generally contain eight lines in each verse.

These strophes are again divided into two halves (vísu-
helmingr) and each of these again into two parts (vísu-
fjorðúngr) which form the fourth part of the whole strophe.

The separate lines or verses (vísuorð) are generally
short, the longest has but four feet, they all have the caesura.

176. The two lines which form the fourth part of the strophe are without exception united by alliteration (letter-rhyme), this is a most essential part of the Icelandic versification. The nature of Alliteration demands that three words should occur in these lines beginning with the same letter. One of these three words must stand at the beginning of the second line and is called the chief letter, the two others in the first line are governed by it, these are called the sub-letters.

If the chief-letter be a compound as -*sp, st* etc., the sub-letters must correspond with it, but if the chief letter be a vowel or a diphthong the sub-letters may change the tone by another vowel, as:

> Stendr Angantýrs
> *au*sinn moldu
> salr í Sámsey
> sunnanverðri.

177. It is not always necessary that the chief-letter stands at the beginning of the line, in short verses it often has a toneless word before it, indispensable for completing the sentence, these are called (málfylling) „*filling up the sentence*", such are *or, sem i* etc.

178. The Assonance or Line-rhyme, consists in the occurrence in the same line of two syllables, the vowels of which and the following cons. agree together. The one stands at the beginning, the other at the end of the syllable. It is called half-assonance when the vowels are different, and only the consonants agree. These two kinds of the Line-rhyme are thus divided; the first line of the quarter verse has the half-assonance, the second has the assonance, as:

held-vild, *in the first line,*
veg-seg, *in the second line.*

179. The final rhyme is the same as in the modern language, except that it is generally monosyllabic, and that the two lines united by the chief-letter rhyme together, as:

> Nú er hersis hefnd
> við hilmi efnd,
> gengr úlfr ok örn
> of Ynglings börn.

180. Quantity is not observed, as all syllables may be long. The freeest and oldest kind of verse is the (fornyrðalag)

speechverse; it has four long syllables, sometimes two with em-
phasis, and if the verse permits it is followed by some short ones.
The example of § 176 is quite regular without short syllables.

181. The Heroic-poems (dróttvæði) generally have the
end-rhyme and the syllabic-rhyme. Regular lines, each with
six long syllables, or three spondees, of which the two first
change with dactyls. This is the verse used in most of the
Sagas. It must be observed, that one meets sometimes a syllable in the oldest verses of this kind, before the chief-letter,
which cannot be looked upon as „málfylling“, but which
belongs to the verse to give it the right lenght, as:

sáttaðu	hrafn i	hausti
of hræ–	solli	gjalla
– ‿ ‿	– –	– –
– –	– –	– –

182. The Songs (rúnhenda) have also regular lines but
they have both syllabic and final rhymes. The shortest verse
of four syllables also has sometimes a syllable before the chief-
letter, for the reason given, as:

við hilmi efnd.

Jon Olafsen, who has written a treatise „on the old Icelandic
Poetry“ expresses the same opinion on pag. 68.

A single short syllable is frequently found in the verse.

PART II.

The Old Norsk Poetry and the Sagas.

Iceland was formerly looked upon as the *ultima Thule* of Virgil; it received the greater part of its population from Norway, where it first became known between the years 860 —870 through the skandinavian navigators N a d d - O d d, G a r - d a r and F l œ k e. The last one called it Iceland in consequence of the masses of drift-ice which he found in all its creeks.

The first settler was the Norweian I n g o l f (870) who fled to the iceland with his retinue and relations from King H a r a l d H á r f a g e r who after having subdued the other petty kings of Norway, obtained supreme power by levelling taxes on all the freeholds of the nobles, whom he in reality reduced to tenants, and all those who would not submit to this usurped authority, emigrated to Iceland, and thus within 60 years the habitable shoreland of the isle was taken possession of.

As most of these emigrants were the freest and noblest men of Norway, some of royal descent, others from the flower of the aristocracy, they continued their old mode of life in their new home, and Iceland became an aristocratic republic. They brought with them their language, the Old Dansk, their rites of heathen worship and their civil institutions. The ground work of their political life was chiefly U l f i l o t's (927), who established a system of law and created the „*Althing*" a national parliament, composed of all the freeholders of the island, which held its meetings every year for 14 days on the great plain of the T h i n g v a l l a to discuss the interests of the land.

Besides this general meeting, there were instituted since 962

a number of smaller Things* for the various districts of the
island, to which was added A. D. 1004 through Njal a superior
court of justice. Christianity, already introduced by some of
the early settlers, was legally established in 1000, and with it
came the knowledge of the latin language and literature, indeed poetry and science found ground ready to receive them
on these shores, and both poetry and historic sagas where already more widely cultivated here than in other parts of the
germanic north.

It is no wonder that in this remote region a literary life
began and literary treasures were kept and reared, whilst the
whole of northern Europe was nothing but a bloody battlefield.
These noble Norsemen had brought with them a beautiful language, diamond-hard, pure as crystal and golden tinted, in
which the Edda Songs were written. We call it the Icelandic
or Old Norsk tongue, but the Old Icelanders called it the
„dönsk túnga och norræna túnga.“

It was once the common language of all the tribes of the
germanic north, spoken in Denmark, Norway, Sweden, The
Faröe, Orkney and Hebrides Islands, and transplanted by the
Danes into England. This tongue is still spoken, with some
modifications, in Iceland and the Faröe Islands, it has kept up
its ancient type, partly from the naturally secluded position of
the island, partly because of its finished literature. In Denmark itself, it underwent a process of degeneration by the mix-
ture with the Anglo-Saxon and German, through the influence
of latin and at last by the french, so that it is scarcely possible
now to trace in the Danish language, the once powerful,
harmonious, full-sounding Norræna-tongue. Thus it is that
since the beginning of the 14th Century, the contrast of the
old-norsk or icelandic tongue (íslendska túnga) and the modern
danish and swedish language has become visible.**

It is interesting to enquire how these rich treasures of
ancient lore were preserved in this remote island. A great
quantity of Sagas matter was collected in Iceland from the very
first, not only did the emigrants bring with them the great
national Sagas of the Norwegians, Swedes and Danes, but also

---

*) Thing in Icelandic means, a meeting or assize, Court of Justice.
**) Koeppen's Literar. Einleitung in die Nordische Mythologie; one
of the best books on icelandic literature and Mythology.
Dietrich's Altnordisches Lesebuch, with Introduction on the Old
Norsk Literature.

the Sagas of the tribes and the local traditions from every part
of Scandinavia; besides a number of Sagas from the other
countries which they continually visited in their numerous
travels by sea and land. The nobles brought with them their
own family Sagas from the remotest times, and they were also
the keepers of the Old Sagas of Gods and Heroes, with the
latter of whom their own families were often connected by
tradition. Hence this incredibly rich mine of poetry and history,
of mythology and superstition in Iceland. Moreover the nobles,
from the old houses of Ynguis or Skiöld, remained in their
northern seats, without any other occupation than the care of
their property, there was little agriculture and that was left to
their servants. The national feasts, and the Things, and also
disputes and wars occasionally interrupted their solitude, otherwise their days glided away evenly enough. Ennui drove the
nobles partly to travel, partly to study and writing, and thus
they became poets and historians, and created this rich icelandic
literature which we possess.

The Skalds.

„The early dawn of literature *) in Europe was almost everywhere else marked by an awkward attempt to copy the classical models of Greece and Rome. In Iceland, an independent
literature grew up, flourished, and was brought to a certain
degree of perfection before the revival of learning in the South
of Europe. This island was not converted to Christianity until
the end of the tenth century, when the national literature,
which still remained in oral tradition, was full blown and ready
to be committed to a written form. With the Romish religion,
latin letters where introduced; but instead of being used, as
elsewhere, to write a dead language, they were adopted by
the learned men of Iceland to mark the sounds, which had been
before expressed by the Runic characters. The ancient language
of the North was thus preserved in Iceland, whilst it ceased to
be cultivated as a written, and soon became extinct as a spoken
language, in the parent countries of Scandinavia.“

The Skalds or poets were the Minnesingers of the North,
they preserved poetry, mythology and history in the verses

---

*) Wheaton's History of the Northmen pag. 49. — an interesting
work for the early history of the Danes and Normans.

which they recited. As early as the 10th Century these icelandic Skalds where known far and near. We find them at
all the northern courts, where they occupy a distinguished position in the trains of kings, whose companions and chroniclers
they were „who liberally rewarded their genius (see Wheaton)
„and sometimes entered the lists with them in trials of skill
„in their own art. A constant intercourse was kept up by
„the Icelanders with the parent country, and the Skalds were
„a sort of travelling minstrels, going continually from one North-
„ern country to another. A regular succession of this order
„of men was perpetuated, and a list of 230 in number, of those
„who were most distinguished in the three Northern kingdoms,
„from the reign of Ragnar Lodbrok to Valdemar II is
„preserved in the Icelandic language, among whom are several
„crowned heads and distinguished warriors of the heroic age.
„The famous king, Ragnar Lodbrok, his queen Aslög or
„Aslauga, and his adventurous sons, who distinguished them-
„selves by their maritime incursions into France and England
„in the ninth century, were all Skalds. A sacred character
„was attached to this calling. The Skalds performed the office
„of ambassadors between hostile tribes, like the heralds of an-
„cient Greece and of the Roman fecial law. Such was the
„estimation in which this order of men was held, that they
„often married the daughters of princes, and one remarkable
„instance occurs of a Skald, who was raised to the vacant
„Jutish throne, on the decease of Frode III, in the fourth Cen-
„tury of the Christian æra.“

In such a position the Skalds accompanied the king in
their raids and to the battle field, they were present in the
banqueting hall and in the hot fight, continually collecting ma-
terials for new Songs, Sagas and Tales; and at last when they
were worn out and tired of life, they returned to their home
in Iceland, frequently covered with renown and with riches,
to tell their friends and countrymen of the foreign countries
they had visited and of their own exploits. The Skalds therefore
much more resemble the knightly Troubadours of the Middle ages
than the Indian Bramahs, or the celtic Druids. They could sing
of fights and battles and deaths, which they had personally wit-
nessed, they could sing of the Sea with its charms and dangers
because they had led a daring Viking life and had steered the
„steed of the sea“; through storms and tempests. They could
sing of the bliss of the Gods and Einheriar, because they

had partaken of kingly hospitality and feasts, the prototype of which was Valhall.

The Skalds obtained their highest position at the time of Eric, the bloody axe, Hacon the Good, Harald and Hacon Jarl.

The most celebrated Skalds of that period were: Egil Skallagrimson, Kormak Augmundarson, Einar Helgason Skalaglam, Eilif Gudrunarson, Guttorm Sindri, Glum Geirason etc., but they were all surpassed by the Norweian Eyvind, the great-grand child of Harald Haarschöns, who received the proud name of Skaldaspillir (the annihilator of the Skalds). Even the Icelanders acknowledged him and sent him a costly present (Harald-Gráfelds-Saga c. 18).*)

„As there were female warriors (Wheaton), or Amazons ,in the heroic age of the North, so there were female Skalds ,or poetesses, whose lays sometimes breathed the harsh notes ,of war and celebrated the achievements of conquering heroes, ,and at others sung the prophetic mysteries of religion.

„Thus we perceive how the flowers of poetry sprung up ,and bloomed amidst eternal ice and snows. The arts of peace ,were successfully cultivated by the free and independent Ice- ,landers. Their Arctic isle was not warmed by a Grecian sun, ,but their hearts glowed with the fire of freedom. The natural ,divisions of the country by ice-bergs and lava streams, insu- ,lated the people from each other, and the inhabitants of each ,valley and each hamlet formed, as it were, an independent ,community. These were again reunited in the general na- ,tional assembly of the Althing, which might not be unaptly ,likened to the Amphyctionic council or Olympic games, where ,all the tribes of the nation convened to offer up the com- ,mon rites of their religion, to decide their mutual differences, ,and to listen to the lays of the Skald, which commemorated „the exploits of their ancestors."

A collection of these early remains of old Scandinavian poetry will be found in the Poetic or Elder Edda, the prose in the Younger Edda and the Sagas, the Njála, the Heimskringla, the Konungsskuggsjá, and the Landnámabók.**)

---

*) A Catalogue of the most celebrated icelandic skalds (Skáldatal) will be found in Worm's Literat. Run, and in Peringskiöld's Edition of the Heimskringla.

**) See Bosworth's Scandin. Literat. with specimens of the va-

Indeed the Icelandic literature begins with the compilation of the Poetic Edda in 1056 and ends in the 14th Century.

The Edda.

In the year 1643 the Bishop of Skalholt Brynjulf Svendsen found amongst other Manuscripts, a very old Membran which contained icelandic poems, he had it copied and added to the title with his own hand „Edda Sæmundar hins Fróda" Edda of Sämund the Wise. The old Manuscript was sent to Copenhagen and is now to be found there in the Royal Library. It seems to have been written in the 14th Century and although not quite perfect, is the chief codex of the Edda.

This Poetic Edda is one of the most incomparable works of the human race, no people have noted down their heathen belief in so innocent a manner and with such freshness of colour as the Icelanders. These Songs are the ancient Relics of Antiquity, and are for the Scandinavian Nations, what Homer and Hesiod combined are for Ancient Greece. It is the thoroughly original and national poetic monument of the Northern Nations.

The Songs of this Edda consist of the Sagas of Gods and Heroes. Edda means „proavia" the great grand mother,* who tells to her numerous grand children the history and tales of their forefathers.

The Songs of the Edda are mythologic or heroic-epic, they are of so remote a period, that it is not likely they were written in Iceland, it is much more probable that they were brought over to Iceland by the old Noble families in whose keeping they were preserved, and it is the proud distinction of the Icelanders that to their intelligence we are indebted for these, the most precious relics of the germanic races.

Wheaton says:**) „About two centuries and a half after „the first settlement of Iceland by the Norwegians the learned „men of that remote island began to collect and reduce to „writing these traditional poems and histories. Sæmund Sig-

---

rious northern Dialects; Mallet's Northern Antiquities. English translations of the Edda by S. Cottle (mythol. songs only) and by Thorpe.

*) Halderson explains: „Módir heitir ein. amma önnur, edda hin þridia." (Moder is called the one [in the first degree] grand mother the second, Edda or the great, grand mother; the third).

**) Northmen page 59.

„fussen, an ecclesiastic, who was born in Iceland in 1056
„and pursued his classical studies in the universities of Ger-
„many and France, first collected and arranged the book of
„songs relating to the mythology and history of the ancient
„North, which is called the poetic, or elder Edda. Various
„and contradictory opinions have been maintained as to the
„manner in which this collection was made by Sæmund, who
„first gave it to the world. Some suppose that he merely
„gathered the Runic manuscripts of the different poems, and
„transcribed them in Latin characters. Others maintain that
„he took them from the mouths of different Skalds, living in
„his day, and first reduced them to writing, they having been
„previously, preserved and handed down by oral tradition
„merely. But the most probable conjecture seems to be, that
„he collected some of this fragmentary poetry from cotem-
„porary Skalds and other parts from manuscripts written after
„the introduction of Christianity and Latin letters into Iceland,
„which have since been lost, and merely added one song of
„his own composition the Sólar Ljód, or Carmen-Solare of
„a moral and Christian religious tendency, so as thereby to
„consecrate and leaven, as it were, the whole mass of paganism."

The Edda contains Ist Songs of the Gods, and IInd Songs
of the Heroes. Völu-spá (the oracle of valá, the seer) tells
of the creation of the World, and the Gods and People who
dwell in it. The Seer has heard of the doings in this world
from her instructors, the primeval giants, and she is acquainted
with nine heavens, she also knows the future.

The entire poem is most prophetic and remarkable.

Grimnis-mál, the Song of Grimnir, in which he de-
scribes the twelve dwellings of the Gods and the splendour of
Valhalla.

The Vafþruðnis-mál, Oðinn undertakes to visit a
wise and powerful giant and to question him on the World,
the Gods and the Giants. The giant gives his replies and
shows his knowledge, but from the tenour of the last question
he guesses that the visitor who has drawn his secrets from him
is the powerful God himself.

The Sólar-liód, the song of the sun, as we have already seen is a christian song, interwoven with old mytholo-
gical fancies.

Besides these four most important songs, the following are
of a very remarkable kind, in which the old poetry has a tinge

of divine lore, namely: the Skirnisför, Vegtamskviða, Harbarðsliöð, Hymiskviða and the Þrymskviða.

The most important of the Songs of the Heroes are the Völundarkviða, the two Songs of Helgakviða, the songs of Sigurð, Tafnismál and Sigrðrifumal.

The Epic contents of some of these Songs are maintained by Jac. Grimm, to have been gathered from the german forefathers, and that the Scandinavians have saved these tutonic remains; these poems are of an epic grandeur, and a truly homeric power, which give them the foremost position in the Edda.

Schools were formed in Iceland in the eleventh Century, and being far distant from Rome, enjoyed much liberty and national formation. The Bishops were elected by the Althing, the schools were not only established in the Monasteries but also in private houses.

The Bishop of Skalholt introduced writing in 1057 and Sagas were then much collected. Without writing there were songs and sagas in abundance, even traditional science, but no literature. The Icelanders like other Norsemen certainly wrote earlier in Runic Characters, but these were only used for inscriptions in wood and stone, to express names, pedigrees and forms of witchcraft, rarely poems.

The Runic alphabet*) „consists properly of sixteen letters, „which are Phenician in their origin. The Northern traditions, „sagas and songs, attribute their introduction to Odin. They „were probably brought by him into Scandinavia, but they have „no resemblance to any of the alphabets of central Asia. All „the ancient inscriptions to be found on the rocks and stone „monuments in the countries of the North, and which exist „in the greatest number near old Sigtuna and Upsala, in Swe-„den, the former the residence of Odin, and the latter of his „successors, and the principal seat of the superstition intro-„duced by him, are written in the Icelandic or ancient Scan-„dinavian language, but in Runic characters.“

The Icelanders first received the latin alphabet from the missionaries, in a double form, namely from the Germans and Anglo-Saxons. The german writing (Mönchsschrift) became however predominant, but they retained some of the anglo-

---

*) Wheaton's Norsemen 61.

saxon characters. — Books were created through school-know-
ledge. Young Icelanders visited Germany, England, Italy and
France to study and prepare themselves for the church; they
studied at the Universities in Oxford, Rome and Paris. Schools
were established to teach christian learning and to educate
their own clergy, Latin, Theology, reading, writing and sing-
ing were the branches chiefly taught.

Sæmund hinn froði, Sigfusson (born 1036. d.
1133) who collected the poetry of the elder Edda had studied
at Paris and Cologne, and in the School on his property Odd
was educated „Snorri Sturluson the author of the Chron-
icles of the Norwegian Kings from Odin downwards, and the
Prose Edda. Historical prose rose to its highest point in the
12th and 13th Centuries when Sagas of all times and countries
were written or translated.

With the gradual fall of the political state in the begin-
ing of the 13th Century, we also find that the compositions
of the Sagas become less numerous; the 14th Century only fur-
nished translations, fictions, fairy tales and Annals, and even
these ceased to be created at the end of the Century, when
Iceland was visited by diseases and plagues.

Poetry of the Skalds.

We find in the 12th Century the most celebrated of the
historical Skalds to be:

Marcus Skeggson, Ivar Ingemundson at the norwegian court, the priest Einarr Skulason court poet, from
1114 with Sigurd in Norway. He wrote poems on Sven, king
of Denmark to whom he went in 1151. In the time of king
Sverrer (1177—1202) the following are the most distinguished
Skalds: Hallr Snorrason, Máni, Blackr, Þorbiörn,
Skackaskald, and the young Snorri Sturluson.

In the first part of the 13th Century Liot, Höskuld
the blind, Jatgeir, Snorri, Jarl Gizur, and chiefly Olaf
hvita skald Þorðarson (d. 1259) the author of the Knytlingasaga and of many poems on king Waldemar of Denmark and Hakon VI of Norway were much esteemed. His
brother Sturla hinn froði (d. 1284) wrote the histories of
Hakon VI and Magnus VII. In the 12th Century we already find
in the Icelandic and Norwegian Sagas a number of folk songs

(Volkslieder) interspersed. Saxo Grammaticus often quotes these songs as authorities.

Prose writing rose high in the 12th Century, historical events were frequently written down, and although the manner in which they were composed, was unfinished, yet an artistic form is visible in the narrative of events and in the treatment of the subjects generally. Real history of which the father is Ari hinn froði who wrote a Chronicle of Iceland, and the Landnámabok is treated too much in the character of dry statistics and genealogy and is much in want of general survey and enlarged handling. It is only when we come to Snorri and his nephews Olaf and Sturla that descriptive history becomes more finished and personal dialogues infuses life into the historical pages. Both Sweden and Norway have taken part in collecting and writing down their old laws and privileges, but we are only indebted to the industry and intelligence of the Icelanders for having preserved to us the traditions of their common Hero Sagas, to which we look as the real history of those remote ages. Without these Sagas there would be a great blank in northern history for several Centuries.

The Sagas.

„The ancient literature of the North" says Wheaton, „was „not confined to the poetical art. The Skald recited the „praises of King and heroes in verse, whilst the Saga-man re- „called the memory of the past in prose narratives. The talent „for story-telling, as well as that of poetical invention, was „cultivated and highly improved by practice. The prince's hall, „the assembly of the people, the solemn feasts of sacrifice, all „presented occasions for the exercise of this delightful art. The „memory of past transactions was thus handed down from age „to age in an unbroken chain of tradition, and the ancient „songs and Sagas were preserved until the introduction of book- „writing gave them a fixed and durable record."

The great mass of Prose writing which has come down to us, from these cold icebound shores, is truly amazing, it contains not only the Sagas of entire tribes, but of kings, Jarls or chiefs, skalds and other celebrities. We will mention some of the most important

Ist Hero Sagas

were one of the first subjects of their prose tales. In the Vol-
sungasaga we find much of the germanic and northern element, it tells of Sigfrid's youthful deeds, this is followed by
the Ragnarlodbrokssaga, in which is set forth how the
danish king, having lost his queen Thora, marries Sigfrid's
daughter, whose sons become the great conquerors. Both Sa-
gas belong to the 12th or beginning of the 13th Century.

The Vilkina or Niflungasaga are based on low german poems and tales.

There are a number of sagas whose heroes are renowned
Icelanders, such as Finnbog and Gretter, Hialmter and
Ölver, Hromund, Hrói and of the swedish Herraud
and Bosi. Styrbiörn, the Swedefighter, Gautrek King
of Westgothia, and of his son Hrolf, and the Sagas of the
Norwegian An, the bow-man, Sturlaug the industrious, Por-
stein the son of Vikings and others.

Foreign Hero-Sagas were introduced into Iceland and Norway during the 13th Century through translations, chiefly by
Hakon Hakonarson and the icelandic clergy; of which
Jón Halltór, Bishop of Skalholt 1322—39 was the most
celebrated. Old British Legends are also early imported through
translations, the Bretasögur is said to have been made by
the monk Gunnlaug Leifson in Thingeyre (1218).

Many foreign sagas were transcribed by order of Hakon
VI, such as the Prophecies of Merlin, the Artursaga, the
Möttulssaga, the monk Robert, the Tristram ok Isod-
dusaga; and in the 13th Century the Alexandrasaga, and
the history of King Tyrus and Pilate, both by Brandr
Jónsson, who died Bishop of Holum in 1264. The precise time
when many of these sagas were translated is not known, as the
Tróamannasaga and the spanish Flor and Blancheflur.

IInd The Historical Sagas

were written unter the title Sögur, they contain much that
is mythic before the time of Halfdan the Black (863) but
much real history is interspersed, which is principally taken
from the pedigrees and traditions of the Nobles of the land. One
of the most important works, on the history of Iceland, chiefly
composed from the various family histories which were then

in existance, is the „Islendingabok“ written by Ari hinn froði (born 1067) which gives a general history of the colonisation and events of the island, down to the beginning of the 12ᵗʰ Century, also the Landnámabók commenced by Ari, which after many continuations was finished by Sturla Pordarson (d. 1284) with additions by Erlauk Erlendson (d. 1334). It contains a complete history of the island from the taking possession of the same to the 10ᵗʰ Century, but it is full of genealogies and dry detail. — We must further mention the excellent Fœreyingasaga (12ᵗʰ C.) which treats of the history of Sigmund, who introduced Christianity into the Farö Islands. The Orkneyingasaga from the middle of the 13ᵗʰ Century; the Heidarvigasaga (12ᵗʰ C.) which gives an account of the battle on the Heath (1013—1015) a fearful contest, in which entire tribes fought against each other. The Hungurvaka (12ᵗʰ Cent.) treats of the first five Bishops of Skalholt.

The Laxdœlasaga (13ᵗʰ Cent.) is an interesting history of the trials and adventures of a very rich norwegian woman Auda, who fled with her father before Harald, first to Scotland and then to Iceland.

The Sturlungasaga (end of the 13ᵗʰ Cent.) is one of the most important historical documents we possess. It begins its narrative in 1110, and relates minutely the fate of Sturle, the father of Snorri, and the various conflicts of his race with other chiefs; its author was Sturla Pordssohn who was engaged in writing it until he went on his journey to Norway in 1164.

The Vigastyrssaga written by a noble Icelander Styr (styled Arngrim) the "murderous fighter"; he was at last slain, and it was in consequence of his death, that the celebrated battle on the Heath was fought.

The Liotsvetninga or Reykdœlasaga, written by the rich Gudmund the powerful (d. 1025) and his sons. It gives an account of the earliest aristocracy of the island (12ᵗʰ C).

The historical biographies of the icelandic Skalds are very interesting. One of the oldest is the Gunnlaug Ormstunga ok Skald Rafn's Saga from the 12ᵗʰ Cent. The Saga of two poets, whose valour was widely renowned is the Fostbrœdrasaga, it tells of Pormod who received his death wound in the battle of Stiklestad, and Porgeir who saw many a fight in Iceland, Ireland, England and Norway,

in the latter country he was for some time Court skald at
Olaf's, until at last he found his end in Iceland, where he
was slain in battle.

The Kormakssaga also belongs to this remarkable kind
of Sagas, in which the battle and love adventures of these
Minnesingers and gallant blades, which they experienced in
their romantic wanderings are told.

The Heimskringla (orbis terrarum) is one of the principal works of Iceland. It is written by Snorre Sturlason, a
man to whom his country's history and literature are much
indebted; and who earned for himself the title of the Northern
Herodotus. A sciou of one of the old noble families, he was
born in the year 1178 at Hvamm. He lived long at the Courts
of Sweden and Norway, became an Icelandic lagman and was
murdered in his castle on the 22nd September 1241. He was
a man of great talents, and made himself famous as a poet,
lawgiver and historian.

Snorre collected 16 Sagas on his numerous voyages, the
first of which treats of the mythic times before Halfdan the
Black, followed by the histories of all Norwegian Kings down
to Magnus Erlingsson (1162—1184). To these are added three continuations; first by Karl Jónsson Abbot of
Thingeyri (d. 1213) who wrote the minute history of King
Sverrer, followed by the histories of Hakon Sverrersson,
Guttorm Sigurðarson and Ingi Bardarson, written by
an unknown author, and lastly by Sturla, the last Skald who
wrote the life of Hakon VI and a fragment of Magnus VII.

Snorre mentions that he has not only used the poems of
the Skalds, but the Sagas of Kings which he found written,
and which he collected in his travels. The completion of the
entire work may be placed towards the year 1230.

With this remarkable book, a masterpiece of history, only
inferior to the Edda itself, closes the history of the Sagas. It
is a mine of Icelandic history and mythology, interesting alike
for its swedish and norwegian Annals, giving at the same
time historical glances at Russia.

The history of the Swedish Kings has not been treated
with originality by the Icelanders; nor has Danish history been
faithfully represented after the 12th Century. The Jomsvikin-
gasaga is the history of the renowned pirates who lived in
the Jomscastle, the terror of navigators and the coast population, and Jarl Hakon's taking and destruction of this Castle;

the Knytlingasaga records the history of Knut the Holy (1080—1086) and his successors down to 1186.

There are also a great number of Biblical Sagas and Old Legends extant, which it would be beside our sketch to dwell upon.

IIIrd The Old Law Statutes.

are of great value to the philologist, as these Old Laws and Statutes were collected and written down by the northern Countries in their own various dialects. One of the oldest is the Icelandic „Grágás" (Greygoose) which name was given to it by its last editor the Lagman Gudmund Þorgeirsson (1123—1135). It commenced in 1119 on the basis of the laws of Ulfliot in the 10th Century, but was only used until the subjugation by Norway, since which time (1273) the Hakonarbók was introduced, which, having being re-edited by Jon an icelandic Lagman (1280) was called Jónsbók.

The Icelandic Cannon-law (Kristinrettr) dates from the year 1275.

IVth Science.

Remains of Learning and Science are not wanting in Iceland, for after the introduction of Christianity, many persons studied abroad. Grammar, Rhetorics, Astronomy, Chronology, Physics and Geography were cultivated by them. The study of Grammar was an especial favourite in which Þorodd became so great that he received the name Runameistari (Grammaticus) but the most celebrated work is the

Younger Edda or Prose Edda.

It was first found 1628 by Arngrim Johnson. Three Codices are extant, two in the Copenhagen and one in the Upsala Library. It was Snorre who contributed mainly to the compilation of this prose Edda.

In the 14th Century the Younger Edda consisted of three parts. The 1st contained the Myths, or the material out of which the poetic language should be formed. The 2nd Kenningar, gave the forms of authority, in which the mythic element should be adopted, and it therefore gives the Mythology of the Poetic Edda. The 3rd part contains the Skalda, the rules or art of poetry adopted by the Skalds subdivided into three classes namely 1) reading and writing, 2) speaking correctly and 3) writing verses as the result of the entire study. It further contains a Dictionary of poetic synonymes and the whole art of versification, alliteration, species of verse, etc.

The „Konungsskuggsiá" Kingsmirror, from the 12ᵗʰ Century, is a curious collection of knowledge and experience. It contains firstly physical and geographical curiosities, secondly, rules of life and manners to be observed in the presence of Kings and Courts, and hence its title.

The learned industry, so long and habitually practised by these noble Icelanders, continued during the Centuries following, but after the introduction of the Reformation, although literary occupations were kept up, the authors wrote in latin, much was translated, nor did poetry entirely die out, but the power and the lustre of its might and beauty were gone, the Saga with its powerful poetry and its heroic elements fled, and the old Icelandic Art was at an end for ever.*)

---

*) We refer the student for further information to
Möbius, T., Ueber die ältere isländische Saga. 1852.
— — Ueber die altnordische Philologie. 1864.
— — Analecta Norrœna. Auswahl aus der isländischen und norwegischen Literatur des Mittelalters. 1859.
These books can be had of the publisher of this Grammar as well as:
Haldorsson's Lexicon Islandico-Latino-Danicum.
Jónsson's Icelandic-Danish Dictionary.
Fritzner, J., Old Norwegian Dictionary.

PART III.
Icelandic Reader.

Sundurlausir Þankar.*)
Sønderløse Tanker.
Separated thoughts.

Icelandic: Gód bók og gód kona, lagfæra margann brest,
Danish: God Bog og god Kone rette mangen Brøst,
English: Good book and good wife mend many fault,

slæm bók og slæm kona skémma margt gott hjartalag, margir
slem Bog og slem Kone forbære mangt godt Hjertelav, mange
bad book and bad wife spoil many good disposition, many

gæta ekki ad ödru á bádum þeim, enn hvörnin þær
see ikke paa andet paa begge dem, end hvorledes de
look not to others on both (sides) them, than how (but only to) they

eru utan; — Fer þeim þá ad kvarta yfir
ere udvortes. — Sømmer dem da at klage over
are the outside (of things). Beseems them then to complain over

hvörnin hid innra seinna reynist.
hvorledes det Indre senere prøves.
how the interior later proves.**)

Heimskum verdur ad halda til góda, þó þeir tali
Dumme bliver at holde til Gode, skjønbt de tale
Stupid must to keep to good, although they speak

nokkra heimsku, því þad væri hardt ad lofa þeim aldrei ad
nogen Dumhed, thi det være haardt at tillade dem aldrig at
some stupidity, for it were hard to allow them never to

tala eitt ord.
tale et Ord.
speak one word.

--- ----

*) From Sivertsen's Icelandic Læsbog.
**) Must be constructed thus: Most people look not to both sides,
but only to the outside of things; it behoves those who complain to
examine both sides.

Correct Danish.

Tantesprog.

En god Bog og en god Kone forbedre mange Feil, en slet Bog og en slem Kone forbærve Manges gode Sindelav. De Fleste see kun paa Begges Udvortes. Sømmer det sig da at klage over hvorledes Begges Indre siden erfares? De Dumme maa man holde det til Gode, skjøndt de tale noget dumt, da det vilde være haardt, aldrig at tillade dem at tale et Ord.

Cátur — Gaader — *Riddles.*

Eg er módurlaus, en hann fadir minn er madurinn minn.
Jeg er moderløs, men han Faber min er Manden min.
I am motherless, but the father my is the husband my.

Frá módur lífi kom eg böfudlaus, og fótavani,
Fra Moder-liv kom jeg hovedbløs, og Føddersmanglende,
From mother's life came I headless and feetwanting,

fell eg þannin mörgum vel, med höfdi og fótum er eg
falder jeg saaledes mange vel, med Hoved og Fødder er jeg
fall I thus many well, with head and feet am I

líka gódur maga þínum, en þá verdur þú ad bída.
ogsaa god Mave din, men da bliver du at vente.
also good [to] stomach thy, but then must thou wait.

Hvad er þad sem í dag ekki verdur þat sama á
Hvad er det som i-dag ikke bliver det samme i-
What is it which to-day not becomes that same to

morgun, missir bord, rum, hús, og nafnid med, en græ-
morgen, mister Bord, Seng, Huus, og Navnet med, men græ-
morrow, loses table, bed, house and the name with but de-

tur þó ekki missirinn.
der dog ikke Skaden (Tabet).
plores yet not the loss.

Correct Danish:

Gaader.

Jeg er moderløs, og min Faber er min Ægtefælle. — Eva.
Jeg er føb uden Hoved og Fødder, og behager dog Mange.

Med Hoved og Føbber smager jeg dig ogsaa ret godt, men saa du maa vente (førend de komme). — Æg.

Hvad er det som i Dag ikke bliver det samme i Morgen, forandrer Bord, Seng, Huus, og maaske Navn, men begræber dog ei Tabet? — en Brud.

Thales — *Thales.*

Merki til heimsku er ofmikil lyst til ad tala.
Mærke paa Dumhed er formegen Lyst til at tale.
Sign of stupidity is too-great desire to to talk.

Likamans farsæld er innifalin í heilbrigdi, en sálar-
Legemets Lyksalighed er indbefattet i Helbred, men Sjæ=
The body's happiness is contained in health, but the

innar i lærdómi.
lens i Lærdom (Kundskab).
soul's in knowledge.

Öl er innri madur.
Øl er indre Mand.
Ale is inner man.

Tyrkja - keisarinn, edur eins og þá var kallad Califen,
Tyrkekeiseren eller lige som da var kalbet Califen,
The Turks' emperor, or as then was called the Calif,

Mahadi var einn af þeim stiórnendum, sem vóru sofandi á
Mahadi var en af de Styrere, som vare sovende paa
Mahadi was one of those rulers, who were sleeping on

kóngs - hásætinu, og feingu ágjörnum rádherrum taum-
Kongs-Høisæbet, og finge gjærrige Raadsherrer Tøm=
the king's-highseat, and delivered avaricious councellors the rein-

haldid i hendur. Einusinni þá hann á dyraveidum var ad
holdet i Hænder. Engang da han paa Dyrefangster var at
keeping in hands. Once then he on deercatchings *was to*
(hunting)

elta steingeit, villtist hann frá fylgiurum sínum, og
forfølge Steengeeb, vildedes han fra Følgere sine, og
pursue stonegoat (went astray) *he from followers his, and*
strayed

nóttin yfirféll hann. Þegar hann var þreyttur ordinn, kom
Natten overfaldt ham. Da han var træt bleven, kom
the night overfell him. When he was tired become, came

hann i riódur, hvar hann sá tjald eitt, úr hvöriu ara-
han i Lund, hvor han saae Telt et, udaf hvilket ara-
he in clearing, where he saw tent a, from which Ara-

biskur madur kom út, og beiddi gést sinn ad vera vel-
bisk mand kom ud, og bad Gjæst sin at være vel-
bic man came out, and asked guest his to be wel-

kominn. Califen lét ekki á bera, hvörr hann væri, annad-
kommen. Califen lob ikke mærke, hvem han var, en-
come. The Calif did not disclose, who he was, ei-

hvört til þess ad sjá seinna hvörnin bónda yrdi vid, þegar
ten til det at see senere hvorlebes Bonde blev ved (teebe sig), da
ther in order to see later how peasant became to, when

hann feingi ad vita, hvör kominn væri, ellegar og hann
han finge at vide, hvo kommen var, eller og han
he got to know, who come was, or also he

ætladi einusinni á lífstíd sinni nióta þess yndis at
agtebe engang paa Livstib sin nybe dets Ynbest (Fornøielses) at
intended once in lifetime his enjoy that delight to

umgángast vid jafninga sinn. Medan þessi ærlegi madur
omgaaes ved Ligemand sin. Medens denne ærlige Mand
converse with his equal. While this honest man

giördi allt hvad hann gat til at taka vel á móti komum-
gjorbe alt hvab han kunde til at tage vel i mob Gjæ-
did all that he could in order to talk well against the com-

anni, spurdi Califen hann ad, hvarfyri hann byggi i
sten, spurgte Califen ham om, hvorfor han byggebe i
er, asked the Calif him about, why he dwelled in

svoddan eydiplátsi? Þadsem þér med svo miklum rétti kallid
svoddan Ødeplads? Detsom De meb saa stor Ret kalber
such desertplace? That which you with so great right call

eydipláts, svaradi hinn arabiski, var fyrrum fjölbyggt
Ødeplads, svarebe hin Arabiske var forbum tætbygget [ted
desertplace, answered the Arab, was formerly numerously inhabi-

af Arabiskum og Tyrkjamönnum, sem höfdu nóg vidurværi
af Arabiske og Tyrke-Mænd, som havde nok Underholb
by Arabs and Turks, who had enough support

af kauphöndlun og akuryrkju, og med ánægin guldæ
af Kjøbhandel og Agerdyrkning, og med Fornøjelse betalte
from trade and agriculture, and with pleasure paid

þolanlegann skatt Califanum Almansor. Sá góði Herra lagdi
taalelig Skat Califen Almansor. Den gode Herre lagde
bearable taxes (to) the Calif Almansor. That good Lord laid

alúd á ad stiórna sínum löndum, og gjöra þegna
Flid paa at styre sine Lande, og gjøre Undersaatter
diligence on to govern his countries and make subjects

sína lukkusæla; en hanns eptirkomara og núverandi
sine lykkelige; men hans Efterkommeres og nuværende
his happy; but his successors and present

stiórnara leti og hyrduleysi hefir feingid hird-
Styreres Dovenskab og Skjødesløshed har givet (Raad-
rulers laziness and carelessness have delivered the coun-

stjórunum í hendur þegna hans, svo ad vegna
styrerne giverne) i Hænder Undersaatter hans, saa at formedelst
cillors in hand subjects his, so that on account

þeirra ágirni eru hinir tvístradir vidsvegar sem hér
beres Gjærrighed ere hine adspredte vide Veie som her
of their avarice are the others scattered far and wide who here

bjuggu ádur. Califen, sem nu í fyrsta sinni heyrdi sannleikann,
byggede før. Califen, som nu førstegang hørte Sandheden,
lived before. The Calif, who now for first time heard the truth,

firtist ekki af þvi, heldur ásetti sér ad verda adgæt-
vrededes ikke af det, men bestemte sig at blive opmærk-
got angry not of it, but resolved himself to be more atten-

nari í embættisskyldu sinni framveigis, en lét ekki
sommere i Embeds-Pligt sin fremdeles, men lod ikke
tive in office-duty his for the future, but let not

húsbóndann á sér merkja med hvada þaunkum hans
Huusbonden paa sig mærke med hvilke Tanker hans
the house-master (on) himself perceive with which thoughts his

sinni var uppfyllt. Sá arabiski vildi gjöra komumanni til
Sind var opfyldt. Den Arabiske vilde gjøre Gjæsten til
mind was upfilled. The Arab would do the comer to

góda allt hvad hann gat, og þó undireins var
Gode alt hvad han formaaede, og dog tillige var
good all what he could, and yet at the same time was

hræddur um ad hann kynni hneixla hann, dró leingi tímann,
bange for at han kunne forføre (støbe) ham, brog længe Timen,
afraid for that he might scandalize him, drew long the time,

ádurenn hann taladi til þess, at hann ætti eina víuflösku,
førenb han talebe til bets, at han eiebe en Biin=Flaffe,
before he spoke to that, that he possessed one wine-flask,

sem hann gjarnan skyldi géfa honum ad drekka úr, ef
som han gjerne ffulbe gibe hannem at briffe af, berfom
which he willingly should give him to drink from, if

géstur þyrdi ad taka þad uppá sína samvitsku, því eptir
Gjæft turbe at tage bet oppaa fin Sambittigheb, thi efter
guest dared to take it upon his conscience, for after

Tyrkja-trú er ekki leyfilegt ad drekka vín, edur neitt sem
Thrffes=Tro er iffe tillabeligt at briffe Biin, eller noget fom
Turks'-religion is not allowable to drink wine, or anything which

áfeingt er. Califen sem var óvanur þessum drikk, vildi
berufenbe er. Califen fom bar ubant benne Drif, bilbe
inebriating is. The Calif who was unused this drink, would

nýta sér tækifærid til at nióta þeirrar ánægiu, sem
nhtte fig Leilighebet til at nhbe bens Fornøjelfes, fom
use for himself the opportunity to to enjoy that pleasure, which

honum var því yndislegri af því hún var fyribodin, og
ham bar befto behageligere af bet hun bar forbuben, og
him was the more delightful because she was forbidden, and

hann vissi ad sitt misbrot mundi hér ei komast upp.
han bibfte at fit Forbrhbelfe monne her ei fommes op.
he knew that his crime would here not come up.

Eptir ad hann var búinn ad drekka hid fyrsta staup, sagdi
Efter at han bar færbig at briffe bet førfte Støb, fagbe
After that he was finished to drink the first glass, said

hann med híru bragdi vid þann arabiska: Minn vin! eg
han meb blibt Aafhn veb ben Arabiffe: Min Ben! jeg
he, with mild mine to the Arab: My friend! I

er einn af hirdsveinum Califans, og þú skalt ei þurfa ad
er en af Hoffbenbe Califens, og bu ffal ei behøve at
am one of courtiers the Calif's and thou shalt not need to

ydrast eptir þann greida sem þú hefir gjört mér. Sá
fortrhbe efter ben Bebærtning fom bu haber gjort mig. Den
repent of that entertainment, which thou hast done me. The

arabiski lét aptur á móti í té gledi og þakklæti
Arabiſke ·lod atter imod i tee Glæbe og (et) Taknemmeligheb
Arab let again in return joy and gratitude

fyri þessa alúd, og syndi komumanni þessmeiri
for denne Opmærkſomhed, og viſte Gjæſten beſtomere
for this condescension, and showed the comer the more

vyrdíngu. Þessi, sem sagdist vera Califans embættismadur,
Anſeelſe. Denne, ſom ſagbes være Califens Embedsmand,
honour. This, who said himself be the Califs officer,

tók fliótt til flöskunnar aptur, en vid hvört eitt staup óx
tog ſnart til Flaſkens atter, men ved hvert et Støb voẋte
took quickly to the bottle again, but at every one glass increased

hans ánægja og vidfeldni. Eg vil ekki leyna þig
hans Fornøjelſe og Omgængeligheb. Jeg vil ikke ſkjule (for) dig
his pleasure and affability. I will not conceal thee

neinu sagdi hann vid húsbóndann, eg er Califans einka
noget ſagbe han ved Huusbonden jeg er Califens bedſte
anything said he to the housemaster, I am the Calif's intimate

vin, sem hann hefir mestar mætur á. Sá vinskapur
Ven, ſom han haver ſtørſte Godheber paa. Den Venſkab
friend whom he has greatest goodness upon. That friendship

sem hann vyrdist at hafa til mín, skal innan skamms géfa
ſom han værdiges at have til mig, ſkal inden Korts give
which he appears to have for me, shall within short give

mér tækifæri at útvega þér velgjördir af hanns hendi.
mig (et) Leiligheb at forſkaffe dig Velgjerninger af hans Haand.
me opportunity to get thee benefits from his hand.

Þegar enn arabiski heyrdi þetta, þóktist hann ei nógsamliga
Da den Arabiſke hørte dette, tyktes han ei nokſomt
When the Arab heard this, thought himself he not sufficiently

géta veitt gésti sínum lotníngu en kysti hanns klædafald,
kunne ybe Gjæſt ſin Højagtelſe men kyſte hans (en) Klæbebon,
be able given guest his reverence but kissed his cloths'-seam,

og beiddi hann fyrir alla muni ad spara ei þetta vín, sem
og bab ham for al Ting at ſpare ei dette Viin, ſom
and bade him by all means to spare not this wine, which

gjördi hann svo lystugann. Mahadi kom sér betur og betur
gjorde ham ſaa lyſtig. Mahadi kom ſig bebre og bebre
made him so merry. Mahadi came himself better and better

í gjæti hjá víninu, svo hann þurfti ekki ad taka nærri
i Venſkab hos Vinet, ſaa han behøvede ikke at tage nær
into friendship by the wine, so that he needed not to take near

sér ad drekka þad fyri húsbóndans bón. Eg sjé sagdi
ſig at brikke bet for Huusbondens Bøn. Jeg ſeer ſagbe
himself to drink it for the housemaster's request. I see, said

hann, ad Öl seigir allann vilja. Eg er hvörki hirdmadur
han, at Øl ſiger al Villje. Jeg er hverken Hoffinbe
he that ale says all will. I am neither courtier

né einka vinur Calífans, heldur er eg Calífen sjalfur, og
eller bebſte Ven Califens, heller er jeg Califen ſelb, og
nor intimate friend of the Calif's, rather am I the Calif himself, and

nú stadfesti eg og ýtreka allt þad loford, sem eg ádur hefi
nu ſtabfæſter jeg og gjentager alt bet Løfte, ſom jeg før har
now confirm I and repeat all that promise which I before have

gjört þér. Arabiski madurinn tók strax í kyrdum frá
gjort big. Arabiſke-manben tog ſtrax i Stilheb fra
made thee. The Arab took immediately in quietness from

honum flöskuna, og ætladi ad bera hana burt. Hvad ertú
hannem Flaſken, og agtebe at bære ben bort. Hvab er bu
him the bottle, and intended to carry her (it) away. What art thou

ad gjöra? spurdi Calífen, sem hugsadi ad sá arabiski mundi
at gjøre? ſpurgte Califen, ſom tænkte at ben Arabiſke monne
to do? asked the Calif, who thought that the Arab would

nú syna sér lángtum meiri lotníngu enn ádur. Þér
nu biſe ſig langt mere Højagtelſe enb før. De
now show him far more reverence than before. You

megit vera hvörhelst sem þér viljid, svaradi húsbóndinn,
maa være hvoſomhelſt ſom De vil, ſvarebe Huusbonben,
may be whosoever which you like, answered the housemaster,

þá læt eg ydur samt ekki drekka meir. Vid fyrsta staupid
ba laber jeg Dem bog ikke brikke meer. Veb førſte Støbet
then let I you yet not drink more. At the first glass

sögdust þér vera stórherra, og því gat eg vel trúad;
ſagbes De være Storherre, og bet kunne jeg vel troet;
thou saidts you were great Lord, and that could I well believe;

vid þad annad vórud þér ordinn mesta uppá hald Calífans,
veb bet anbet var De bleben meſte Afholb Califens,
at the second were you become greatest favourite of the Calif's,

og þá hafdi eg stóra vyrdingu fyrir ydur; vid hid þridja
og da havde jeg ftor Ærbødigfed for Dem; ved det tredie
and then had I great reverence for you; at the third

sögdust þér vera Calífen sjálfur, og þad getur skéd,
fagdes De være Califen felv, og det fan flee,
thou saidst you were the Calif himself, and that may happen

ad þad sé satt; en hætt er vid, ad þér vid fjórda staupid
at det er fandt; men farligt er ved, at De ved fjerde Støbet
that it be true; but danger is to, that you at the fourth glass

segist vera okkar stóri spámadur Mohameth, og kannské
figes være vores ftore Spaamand Mohamed, og fanflee
say you were our great prophet Mahometh, and perhaps

vid fimta staupid almáttugur Gud; en því á eg bágt med
ved femte Støbet almægtige Gud; men det ejer jeg Ondt med
at the fifth glass Almighty God; but that own I difficult with

ad trúa. Mahadi hló ad þessu einfaldlega en þó ekki
at troe. Mahadi loe ad dette eenfoldige men dog ifke
to believe. Mahadi laughed at this simple but yet not

heimskuliga svari; og þar vínid var farid ad stíga uppi
dumme Svar; og da Vinet var faret at ftige op i
stupid answer; and as the wine was begun to rise up in

höfudid, lagdi hann sig nidur á ábreiduna, sem hús-
Hovedet, lagde han fig ned paa Teppen, fom Huus-
the head, laid he himself down on the coverlet, which the house-

bóndinn hafdi ætlad honum til sængur um nóttina. Daginn
bonden havde agtet ham til Sengs om Natten. Dagen
master had intended (for) him as bed during the night. The day

eptir reid hann af stad, tók med sér þann arabiska, svo sem
efter reed han affted, tog med fig den Arabifke, faafom
after rode he away, took with him the Arab, as

leidsögumann, og gaf honum stór gjafir, þegar þeir komu
Ledfagelfesmand og gav ham ftore Gaver, da de kom
guide and gave him great presents, when they came

til Bagdad.
til Bagdad.
to Bagdad.

Utlegdarsagan.

Gódgjördasamur madur nokkurr ásetti sér ad audsyna velgjördir einum þræli sínum, gaf honum þessvegna frelsi, skip med öllum reida, og svo mikinn forda, sem nógur væri til ad leita sér lukku og frama med, í hvöriu hellst landí sem hann vildi taka sér bólfestu. Þessi frelsíngi fór um bord, og lét úr lagi, en skelfilegr stormur kom uppá, sem hrakti hann uppa nokkra ey, er honum syndist vera óbygd. Nú var hann búínn ad missa allt hvad hann átti, hjálpárlaus, vissi ekkert hvad af sér mundi verda, og gat ei hugsad til seinni timanna án skélfíngar. Hann var einsog í þoku hvad hann átti ad horfa, gékk áfram í þaunkum, edur réttara ad seigja þánkaleysi, þángadtil fyri honum vard slèttur og trodinn vegur. Med gledi héllt hann áfram þann veg, og sá áleingdar stóra borg, hvad ed jók hans fögnud, svo hann hvatti sporid til ad koma þángad sem fliótast. Hissa vard hann, þegar hann nálgadist borgina, sá hennar innbyggjara koma í hópatali á móti sér, segja sig velkominn med mestu blidlátum, og ad stadarins túlkur hrópadi harri röddu: þessi er ydar Kòngur! Allir fylgdu honum til borgarinnar med fögnudi og gledilátum; hann var leiddur med mestu vidhöfn og prakt í þá höll, hvar Kóngarnir vóru vanir ad hafa sitt adsetur, var færdur í purpura kápu og dírmæt kóróna sett á hans höfud. Ædstu höfdíngjar borgarinnar sóru honum hollustu eid í alls lídsins nafni, ad þeir skyldu vera honum hlídnir, hollir, og trúir, einsog þeim bæri vid Kóng sinn ad breyta. Sá nýi Kóngur hugsadi í fyrstunni, ad þetta allt væri ekki annad enn draumur, en af reynslunni hlaut hann ad gánga úr skugga um, ad þetta var raunar einsog þad syndist, svo hann í huganum vard ad spyrja siálfinn sig; hvad á þetta ad þýda? Og hvad mun sá ædsti Stiórnari allra hluta ætla sér med mig? Þessi þánki fór aldrei úr huga hans, og

Audsyna, *show.*
Fordi, *provisions.*
leita, *search.*
Frami, *honour.*
Bólfesta, *dwelling.*
ad lata úr lagi, *to leave the harbour.*
hrakti, *drifted.*
búinn, *finished.*
án, *without.*

horfa, *apply.*
áleingdar, *from distance.*
hvatti sporid, *quickened his paces*
hárri röddu, *in a loud voice.*
Adsetur, *residence.*
dírmætr, *precious.*
breyta, *behave.*
hlaut, *was obliged.*
gánga úr skugga, *be convincèd.*
raunar, *really, in fact.*

6*

loksins kom hann honum til ad grendslast eptir, hvornin á öllu þessu stædi. Hann kalladi því þann af hirdmönnum sínum fyri sig, sem optast var vanur ad vera í kríngum hans persónu, var hans rádaneyti, og sem af Guds forsjón syndist hafa verid settr honum til adstodar í landstjörninni. Dróttseti! sagdi hann: hvörr hefur gjört mig ad ykkar Kóngi? hvorsvegna hlýda mér allir? og hvad á af mér ad verda? Vitid Herra, svaradi hirdst jórinn honum, ad innbyggendur eyar þessarar, hafa bedid Gud ad senda þeim á ári hvöriu þann Kong sem sé af Adám kominn. Sá Almáttugi hefur bænheirt þá, svo ad á ári hvöriu kemur híugad ein manneskja, allur lídurinn tekur med mestu vidhöfn og fögnudi móti þessum manni, og setur hann til Kóngs yfir sig; en hans ríkisstjórn varir ekki leingur enn eitt ár. Þegar sá tími er á enda, þá er honum velt úr hásætinu, dregin af honum tignar klædin, og hann aptur færdur í lítilfjorliga larfa, strídsmenn, sem ekki géfa nein grid, færa hann ofan til strandar, og kasta honum þar úti skip, er flytur hann til annarar eyar, sem af siálfrar sinnar kostum er hrióstrug og gædalaus. Sásem fyri nokkrum dögum var ríkur kóngur, hefur þá hvorki Þegna né vini, en lifir þar í sorg og eymd. Lídurinn, sem laus er ordinn vid sinn gamla Kóng, flýtir sér þá ad medtaka þann nýa, sem Guds forsjón árlega sendir híngad, og þetta Herra! er þad óumbreytanlega lögmal, sem ekki stendur í ydar valdi ad raska. Vissu þeir sem fyri mig hafa verid spurdi Kóngurinn, þessi hördu forlög? Eingum þeirra svaradi Dróttsetinn, hefir þad verid dulid, en þeir hafa ei haft nógann mód og mannshug ad athuga svo sorglegar Útfarir, þar augu þeirra hafa verid blindud af glampa Kongdæmisins. Þeir hafa lifad og látid einsog vellystíngar og ánægja hafa hvatt þá til, og aldrei hugsad til ad ná stödugri lukku, eda gjöra sér bærileg þau endalok, sem þeir vissu sér var ómögulegt ad umflýa; þeirra lukku ár leid ætid fliótara enn þá vardi, svo ófara dagurinn kom loksins yfir þá fyrr enn þeir vóru búnir, ad búa nokkud í haginn fyri sig, ad eymd og útlegd þeirra yrdi þeim bærileg. Þegar Kongurinn heyrdi þetti, vard hann miög óttasleginn, sveid honum þad mest, ad mikill partur af dírmæta timanum var til ónýtis lidinn; hann ásetti sèr því ad brúka þess betur

grendslast eptir, *inquire.*
adstod, *assistance.*
Dróttseti, *counsellor.*
lítilfjörlegr, *mean.*
larfar, *rags.*

hrióstrugur, *barren.*
Þegn, *subject.*
eymd, *distress.*
óumbreytanlegr, *unalterable.*
raska, *alter.*

það af honum, sem eptir var. Þú vitri Dróttseti! Sagdi hann til hans, þú hefir sagt mér mitt tilkomandi ófall, segdu mér líka hvört medal er til ad komast klaklaust hjá því? Minnist þér, Herra! svaradi Drótisetinn, ad þér komud hingad allslaus til eyarinnar, og athugid þá undir eins ad allt eins muni verda, þegar þér farid hédan, og ad þér aldrei munud siá hana aptur. Eitt einasta medal er til, ad varna því ófalli sem fyrir ydur liggur, þér verdid ad senda smidi til eyarinnar, sem þér egid ad fara til, láta byggja þár stór vistahús, og fylla þau af öllu sem þarf til vidurlífis. Forsómid hédanaf ekkert augnablik sem þéna kann til ydar lukku og brúkid öll þau medöl sem þér gétid upphugsad, til ad koma í veg fyri þá vesöld, sem fliótt dynur yfir en leingi varir; allt þetta verdur ad giörast undandráttarlaust því tídin flýgur, sá fastsetti tímans púnktur nálgast, og það er forgéfins ad ætla sér ad aptur kalla þá stund sem aflifud er; en yfir alla hluti fram, munid til þess ad á þeim stad, sem þér egid til svoddan lángframa ad búa, munud þér ekkert fyri finna nema það, sem þer látid flytja þangad, á þeim stutta tíma er þér egid ennu eptir. Kóngurinn féllst á rád Dróttseta síns, sendi strax smidi til Eyarinnar ad koma öllu þessu í verk, hann lét gjöra eyuna ad yndisligum og gagnlegum bústad. Loksins kom sá ákvardadi dagur, kónginum var snarad úr hásætinu, allur Kóngs-skrúdi af honum tekinn, og hann hnepptur útí skip sem flutti hann i hans Utlegdarstad. Þessi afsetti Kóngur kom þángad lukkulega, og lifdi þar bædi rólegri og ánægdari enn ádur.

ófall, *disaster*.	vidurlifi, *subsistence*.
Klaklaust, *without danger*.	undandráttarlaust, *without delay*.
Vistahus, *store-room*.	lángframa, *for so long a time*.

Af Egils-Saga.

Upphaf rikis Haralds hárfagra.

Haraldr, son Hálfdánar svarta, hafði tekit arf eptir föður sinn; hann hafði þess heit streingt, at láta eigi skera hár sitt ne kemba, fyrr en hann væri einvaldskonúngr yfir Noregi; hann var kallaðr Haraldr lúfa.

Síðan barðist hann við þá konúnga, er næstir váró, ok

sigraði þa, og eru þar lángar frásagnir. Síðan eignaðist hann Upplönd, þaðan fór hann norðr í Þrándheim, ok átti þar margar orrostur, áðr hann yrði einvaldi yfir öllum Þrændalögum.

Siðan ætlaði hann at fara norðr í Naumudal á hendr þeim brœdrum Herlaugi ok Hrollaugi, er þá váro konúngar yfir Naumudal. En er þeir brœdr spurðu til ferðar hans, þá gekk Herlaugr í haug þann með tólfta mann, er áðr höfðu þeir gera látið, ok váro at þrjá vetr; var siðan haugrinn aptrlokinn. En Hrollaugr konúngr veltist or konúngdómi, ok tók upp jarlsrètt, ok fór síðan á vald Haralds konúngs, ok gaf upp ríki sitt. Svá eignaðist Haraldr konúngr Naumdœlafylki ok Hálugaland; setti hann þar menn yfir ríki sitt.

Síðan bjóst Haraldr konúngr or Þrándheimi með skipaliði, ok fór suðr á Mœri, átti þar orrostu við Húnþjóf konúng, ok hafði sigr; fèll þar Húnþjófr: þá eignaðist Haraldr konúngr Norðmœri ok Raumsdal.

En Sölvi klofi, son Húnþjófs, hafði undan komizt, ok fór hann á Sunnmœri til Arnviðar konúngs, ok bað hann ser fulltíngs, ok sagði svá: Þótt þetta vandrædi hafi nú borit oss at hendi, þa mun eigi lángt til, at sama vandrædi mun til yðvar koma; þvíat Haraldr ætla ek at skjótt mun her koma, þa er hann hefir alla menn þrælkat ok áþjáð, sem hann vill á Norðmœri ok í Raumsdal. Munu þer hinn sama kost fyrir höndum eiga, sem vær áttum, at verja fe yðvart ok frelsi, ok kosta þartil allra Þeirra manna, er yðr er liðs af van, ok vil ek bjóðast til með mínu liði móti þessum ofsa ok ójafnaði. En at öðrum kosti munu þer vilja taka upp Þat ráð, sem Naumdœlir gerðu, at gánga með sjálfvilja í ánauð, ok gerast þrælar Haralds. Þat þótti föður mínum sigr, at deyja í konúngdómi með sœmd, heldr en gerast undirmaðr annars konúngs á gamals aldri: hygg ek at þer muni ok svá þykja, ok öðrum þeim er nokkurir ero borði, ok kappsmenn vilja vera. Af slíkum fortölum var konúngrinn fastráðinn til þess at samna liði, ok verja land sitt.

Bundu þeir Sölvi þá saman lag sitt, ok sendu orð Auðbirni konúngi, er rèð fyrir Firðafylki, at hann skyldi koma til liðs við þa. En er sendimenn komu til Auðbjarnar konúngs, ok báru hánum þessa orðsendíng, þá rèðst hann um við vini sína, ok rèdu hánum þat allir, at samna liði, ok fara til móts við Mœri, sem hánum váro orð send til.

Auðbjörn konúngr lèt skera upp herör, ok fara herboð um allt sitt ríki; hann sendi ok orð ríkismönnum, ok bað þá

koma á sinn fund. En er sendimenn konúngs komu til Kveld-
Úlfs, ok sögðu hánum sín erendi, ok þat at konúngr vill, at
Kveld-Úlfr komi til hans með alla húskarla sína; þá svarar
hann: Þat mun konúngi skylt þykja, at ek fara með hánum,
ef hann skal verja land sitt, ok se herjat í Firðafylki, en hitt
ætla ek mer allóskylt at fara norðr á Mœri ok berjast þar, ok
verja land þeirra. Er yðr þat skjótast at segja, þá er þer hittið
konúng yðvarn, at Kveld-Úlfr mun heima sitja um þetta her-
hlaup, ok hann mun eigi herliði samna, ok eigi gera sína þá
heimanferð, at berjast móti Haraldi lúfu; þvíat ek hygg at hann
hafi þar byrði gnóga hamíngju, er konúngr várr hafi eigi krep-
píng fullan. Fóro sendimenn heim til konúngs, ok sögðu hánum
erendislok sín, en Kveld-Úlfr sat heima at búum sínum.

Þeir Þórólfr ok Egill váro þann vetr með. Þóri (hersi)
í góðu yfirlæti, en um várit bjuggu þeir lángskip mikit, ok
fengu manna til, fóru um sumarit í Austrveg ok herjuðu, fengu
þar of fjár, ok áttu orrostor margar. Þeir héldu til Kúrlands,
ok lögðu við landsmenn hálfs mánaðar frið, ok höfðu við þá
kaupstefnu; en er því var lokit, þá tóko þeir at herja, ok lögðu
at í ýmsum stöðum.

Einn dag lögðu þeir at við árós einn mikinn, ok var þar
mörk mikil á land upp; þeir réðu þar til uppgöngu. Liði var
skipt í sveitir, tólf mönnum saman; þeir gengu yfir skóginn,
ok var þá eigi lángt, áðr en bygðin tók vid; þeir ræntu þá,
ok drápu menn, en liðit flýði, unz þeir fengu önga viðtöku.
En er áleið daginn, þá lèt Þórólfr blása liðinu til ofangöngu;
sneru menn þá aptr á skóginn, þar sem hverr var staddr. En
er þeir Þórólfr rannsökuðu liðit, þá var Egill eigi ofankominn,
ok sveit hans, en þá tók at myrkva af nótt, ok þóttust menn
eigi mega leita hans.

Egill hafði gengit yfir skóg nokkurn, ok tólf menn með
hánum, ok sá þeir þá slèttur myklar ok bygðir. Bœr einn
stóð skamt frá þeim; þeir stefna til bœjarins, en er þeir komo
þar, hlaupa þeir í hús inn, ok verða ekki við menn varer;
þeir tóko fe þat allt, er fyrir þeim var, laust, þar váro mörg
hús, ok dvaldist þeim þar lengi.

En er þeir váro útkomnir, ok frá bœnum, var lið komit
milli þeirra ok skógarins, ok sótti þat at þeim. Skíðgarðr var
hár frá bœnum til skógarins; þá mælti Egill, at þeir skyldu
fylgja hánum, svá at eigi mætti öllum megin at þeim gánga.
Þeir gerðu svá, gekk Egill fyrstr, en síðan hverr at öðrum,
svá nær at ekki mátti skilja þá. Kúrer sóttu at þeim fast, ok

mest með lögum ok skotum, en gengu ekki í höggorrostu. En er þeir Egill héldu fram með skíðgarðinum, fundu þeir eigi fyrr, en þar gekk annarr skíðgarðr jafnframt, ok gerðist þar mjótt í milli, þartil er lykkja varð á, ok mátti eigi framkomast. Kúrir sóttu eptir þeim í kvína, en sumir sóttu utan at, ok lögðu spjótum ok sverðum í gegnum garðana, en sumir báru klæði á vápn þeirra. Urðu þeir Egill sárer, ok því næst handtekner, ok aller bundner, leiddir svá heim til bœjarins.

Sá var ríkr maðr ok auðigr, er bœ þann átti; hann átti son roskinn. Þá var umrœdt, hvat við þá skyldi gera: sagði bóndi, at hánum þótti þat ráð, at drepinn, væri hverr á fœtr öðrum; bóndason segir at þá gerði myrkt af nótt, ok mátti enga skemtan af hafa at kvelja þá, bað hann láta bíða mörgins. Var þeim þá skotið í hús eitt, ok bundnir ramliga; Egill var bundinn við staf einn, bæði hendr ok fœtr; síðan var húsit læst ramliga, en Kúrir gingu inn í stufu, ok mötuðust, ok váro allkátir ok drukku.

Egill fœrðist við, ok treysti stafinn, til þess er upplosnaði or gólfinu; síðan féll stafrinn, smeygðist Egill þá af stafnum. Eptir þat leysti hann hendr sínar með tönnum; en er hendr hans voru lausar, leysti hann bönd af fótum ser. Síðan leysti hann felaga sína; en er þeir váro aller lauser, þá leituðust þeir um, hvar líkast var út at komast. Húsit var gert at veggjum af timbrstokkum stórum, en í annan enda hússins var skjaldþili flatt, hljópu þeir þarat, ok brutu þilit; var þar hús annat, er þeir komo í, váro þar ok timbrveggir um.

Þá heyrðu þeir manna mál undir fœtr ser niðr; leituðust þeir þá um, ok fundu hurð í gólfinu, luku þeir þar up, var þarundir gröf djúp, heyrðu þeir þángat manna málit. Þá spurði Egill hvat manna þar væri. Sá nefndist Áki, er við hann mælti. Egill spurði ef þeir vildi upp ur gröfinni; Áki segir at þeir vildu þat gjarna; síðan létu þeir Egill síga festi ofan í gröfina, þá er þeir váro bundnir með, ok drógu þar upp þrjá menn. Áki segir at þat váro synir hans tveir, ok þeir váro menn dansker, höfðu þar orðit hertekner it fyrra sumar. Var ek, sagði hann, vel haldinn í vetr, hafða ek mjök fjárvarðveizlur búanda, en sveinarner váro þjáðer ok undu þeir ílla. Í vár réðu ver til, ok hlupum á brott, ok urðum síðan fundner, váro ver þá her setter í gröf þessa. Þer mun her kunnigt um húsaskipan, segir Egill, hvar oss er vænst á brott at komast. Áki sagði at þar var annat skjaldþili: brjóti þer þat upp, munu þer þá koma fram í kornhlöðu, en þá er út-gánga sem sjálfr vill. Þeir Egill gerðu svá, brutu upp þilit, gengu síðan í hlöðuna, ok þaðan út. Niðamyrkr var á. Þá mæltu þeir förunautar Egils, at þeir skyldu skunda á skóginn. Egill mælti við Áka ef þer eru her kunnig hýbýli, þá muntu vìsa oss til fefanga nokkurra. Áki segir at eigi mundi þar skorta lausafe: her er lopt mikit, er bóndi sefr í, þar skorter eigi vápn inni. Egill bað þá þángat fara til loptsins; en er þeir komo upp á loptriðit, þá sá þeir at loptit var opit; var þar ljós inni, ok þjónostu-menn, ok bjuggu rekkjur manna. Egill bað þá suma úti vera, ok gæta at engi kæmist út. Egill hljóp inn í loptit, greip þar vápn, þvíat þau skorti þar eigi inni, drápu þar menn alla, þá er þar váro inni; þeir tóko ser aller alvæpni.

Áki gekk þar til er hlemmr var í gólfþilinu, ok lauk upp, mælti at þeir skyldi þar ofan gánga í undirskemmuna. Þeir tóko ser ljós, ok gengu þángat; váro þar fehirzlur bónda ok griper góðer ok silfr mikit; tóko men ser þar byrðar, ok báru út. Egill tók undir hönd ser mjöddrekku eina vel mikla, ok bar hana undir hendi ser. En er þeir komo í skóginn, þá nam Egill stað ok mælti: þessi ferð er allíll, ok eigi hermannlig; ver höfum stolit fe bónda, svá at hann veit ekki til, skal oss aldregi þá skömm henda; förum nú aptr til bœjarins, ok látum þá vita hvat títt er. Allir mæltu því í mót, sögðu at þeir vildu til skips.

Egill setr niðr mjöðdrekkuna, síðan hefr hann á rás, ok rann til bœjarins; en er hann kom til bœjarins, þá sá hann, at þjónostusveinar gengu frá eldaskála með skutildiska, ok báru inn í stofuna. Egill sá at í eldahúsinu var eldr mikill, ok katlar yfir, gekk hann þángat til. Þar höfðu verit stokkar stórer flutter heim, ok svá eldar gerver, sem þar er siðvenja til, at eldinn skal leggja í stoksendann, ok brennr svá stokkrinn. Egill greip upp stokkinn, ok gekk heim til stofunnar, ok skaut þeim endanum er logaði upp undir upsina, ok svá upp í næfrina, ok festi þar eldinn í skjótt. En viðir láu þar skamt ì brott, ok bar hann þá fyrir stofudyrnar. Eldrinn las skjótt tróðviðinn, en þeir er við drykkjuna sátu; fundu eigi fyrr, en loginn stóð inn um ræfrit. Hljópo menn þá til dyranna; en þar var ekki greiðfœrt út, bæði fyrir viðunum, svá þat at Egill varði dyrnar, ok drap þá flesta er út leituðu, bæði í dyrunum ok úti fyri.

Bóndi spyrr, hverr fyrir eldinum réði. Egill segir: sá einn ræðr nú fyrir eldi, er þer mundi ólíkast þykja í gærkveld, ok skaltu ekki beiðast at baka heitara, en ek mun kinda; skaltu hafa mjúkt bað fyrir mjúka rekkju, er þú veitter mer ok mínum förunautum. Er her nú sá sami Egill, er þú lézt fjötra, ok binda við stafinn í húsi því, er þer læstuð vandliga: skal nú launa þer viðtökur, sem þú ert verðr. Í því ætlar bóndi at leynast út í myrkrit, en Egill var nærstaddr, ok hjó hann þegar banabögg, ok marga aðra. En þat var svipstund ein, aðr stufan brann, svá at hon féll ofan; týndist þar mestr hluti liðs þess, er þar var inni.

En Egill gekk aptr til skógarins, fann þar förunauta sína, fara þá allir saman til skips. Sagði Egill, at mjöðdrekku þá vill hann hafa at afnámsfe, er hann fór með, en hon var reyndar full af silfri. Þeir Þórólfr urðu allfegnir, er Egill kom ofan, héldu þeir þá þegar frá landi, er mornaði. Áki ok þeir feðgar váro í sveit Egils. Þeir sigldu um sumarit, er áleið, til Danmarkar, ok lágu þar enn fyri kaupskipum, ok ræntu þar er þeir komust við.

Haraldr Gormsson hafði þá tekit við ríki í Danmörk, en Gormr var þá dauðr', faðir hans; landit var þá herskátt, lágu víkíngar mjög úti fyri, Danmörku. Áka var kunnigt í Danmörku bæði á sjá ok landi; spurði Egill hann mjög eptri, hvar þeir staðer væri, er stór fefaung mundi fyriliggja. En er þeir komu í Eyrarsund, þá sagði Áki at þar var á land upp kaupstaðr mikill, er hèt í Lundi, sagði at þar var feván, en líkligt at þar mundi vera viðtaka, er bœjarmenn væri. Þat mál var uppborit fyri liðsmönnum, hvárt þar skyldi ráða til uppgaungu eða eigi. Menn tóko þar allmisjafnt á, fýstu sumer en sumer löttu, var því máli skotið til stýrimanna. Þórólfr fýsti heldr uppgaungu; þá var rœdt við Egil, hvat honum þótti ráð hann kvað visu:

Upp skolum orum sverðum,
úlfs-tann-lituðr! glitra;
eigum dáð at drýgja
í dal miskunn fiska.
Leiti upp til Lundar
lýða hverr sem bráðast;
gerum þar fyri setr sólar
seið ófagran vigra.

Síðan bjuggust menn til uppgaungu, ok fóro til kaupstaðarins. En er bœjarmenn urðu varer við úfrið, þá stefndu þeir í mót; var þar treborg um staðinn, settu þeir þar menn til at verja; tókst þar bardagi hinn harðasti. Egill sótti at hliðinu fast með sína sveit, ok hlífði ser litt; varð þar mikit mannfall; því at hverr fèll um annan borgarmanna. Er svá sagt at Egill gengi fyrstr manna í borgina, ok síðan hverr at öðrum; síðan flýðu bœjarmenn, var þar mannfall mikit. En þeir Þórólfr ræntu kaupstaðinn, ok tóku mikit fe, en brendu bœjinn, áðr þeir skildust við. Fóro síðan ofan til skipa sinna.

Af Snorre Sturlesens Heimskríngla.

Saga Hákonar góða.

1. Hákon Aðalsteinsfóstri var þá á Englandi, er hann spurði andlát Haralds konúngs föður síns; bjóst hann þá þegar til ferðar: fèkk Aðalsteinn konúngr hánom lið, ok góðan skipakost, ok bjó hans för allvegliga; ok kom hann um haustit til Noregs. Þá spurði hann fall brœðra sinna, ok þat með at Eiríkr konúngr var þá í Víkinni: sigldi þá Hákon norðr til Þrándheims, ok fór á fund Sigurðar Hlaðajarls, er allra spekínga var mestr í Noregi, ok fèkk þar góðar viðtökur, ok bundo þeir lag sitt saman; hèt Hákon hánom miklo ríki, ef hann yrði konúngr. Þá lèto þeir stefna þíng fjölmennt, ok á þíngino talaði Sigurðr jarl af hendi Hákonar, ok bauð bóndom hann til konúngs. Eptir þat stóð Hákon sjálfr upp ok talaði; mælto þá tveir ok tveir sín á milli, at þar væri kominn Haraldr hárfagri, ok orðinn úngr í annat sinn. Hákon hafði þat upphaf síns máls, at hann beiddi bœndr viðtöku, ok at gefa ser konúngsnofn, ok þat með at veita ser fulltíng ok styrk til at halda konúngdómiuom; en þarímót bauð hann þeim at gera alla bœndr óðalborna, ok gefa þeim óðol sín, er áðjoggu. At þesso örendi varð rómr svá mikill, at allr bónda múgrinn œpti ok kallaði, at þeir vildi hann til konúngs taka; ok var svá gert, at Þrændir tóku Hákon til konúngs um allt land, [þar var hann 15 vetra: tók hann ser þá hirð, ok fór yfir land.

Þau tíðindi spurðust á Upplönd, at Þrændir höfðo ser konúng tekit, slíkan at öllu sem Haraldr hinn hárfagri var, nema þat skildi, at Haraldr hafði allan lyd í landi [þrælkat ok áþjáð, en þessi, Hákon, vildi hverjom manni gott, ok bauð aptr at gefa bóndom óðöl sín, þau er Haraldr konúngr hafði af þeim tekit. Við þau tíðindi urðo allir glaðir, ok sagði hverr öðrum, flaug þat sem sinoeldr allt austr til lands enda. Margir bœndr fóro af Upplöndum at hitta Hákon konúng; sumir sendo menn, sumir gerðo orðsendíngar ok jartegnir, en allir til þess, at hans menn vildo gerast. Konúngr tók því þakksamliga.

2. Hákon konúngr fór öndurðan vetr á Upplönd, stefndi þar þíng, ok dreif allt fólk á hans fund, þat er komast mátti; var han þá til konúngs tekinn á öllum þíngom; fór hann þá austr til Víkr.

11. Þá er Hákon var konúngr í Noregi var friðr góðr með bóndom ok kaupmönnum; svá at engi grandaði öðrum ne annars fe; þá var ok ár mikit bæði á sjá ok landi. Hákon konúngr var allra manna glaðastr ok málsnjallastr ok lítillátastr; hann var maðr stórvitr, ok lagði mikinn hug á lagasetníng: hann setti Gulaþíngslög með raði Þorleifs spaka; ok hann setti Frostaþíngslög með ráði Sigurðar jarls ok annarra þrænda, þeirra er vitrastir váro; en Heiðsæfislög hafði sett Hálfdán svarti, sem fyrr er ritat.

15. Hákon konúngr var vel kristinn, er hann kom í Noreg, en fyrir því at þar var land allt heiðit, ok blótskapr mikill, ok stórmenni mart; en hann þóttist liðs þurfa mjök ok alþýðu vinsæld; þá tók hann þat ráð, at fara leyniliga með kristninni, hèlt sunnodaga ok frjádagafösto ok minníng hinna stœrsto hátíða. Hann setti þat í lögom, at hefja jólahald þann tíma, sem kristnir menn, ok skyldi þá hverr maðr eiga mælis öl, en gjalda fe ella, ok halda heilagt meðan öl ynnist; en áðr var jólahald hafit Höko-nótt, þat var miðsvetrar nótt, ok haldin þriggja nátta jól. Hann ætlaði svá, er hann festist í landino, ok hann hefði frjálsliga undir sik lagt allt landit, at hafa þá fram kristniboð. Hann gerði svá fyrst, at hann lokkaði þá menn, er hánom váro kærstir til kristni; kom svá með vinsæld hans, at mjök margir lèto skírast, en sumir lèto af blótom. Han sat löngom í Þrándheimi, þvíat þar var mestr styrkr landsins. En er Hákon konúngr þóttist fengit hafa 'styrk af nokkorum ríkismönnum, at halda upp kristninni, þá sendi hann til Englands eptir biskupi ok öðrum kennimönnum; ok er þeir komu í Noreg, þá gerði Hákon konúngr þat bert, at hann vildi bjóða kristni um allt land, en Mœrir ok Raumdœlir skuto þannug síno máli, sem Þrændir váro. Hákon konúngr lèt þá vígja kirkjor nokkorar, ok setti þar presta til. En er hann kom í Þrándheim, þá stefndi hann þíng við bœndr, ok bauð þeim kristni. Þeir svara svá, at þeir vilja þesso máli skjóta til Frostaþíngs, ok vilja þá at þar komi menn or öllum fylkjom, þeim sem ero í Þrænda lögom; segja at þá máno þeir svara þesso vandmæli.

17. Hákon konúngr kom til Frostaþíngs, ok var þar komit allfjölmennt af bóndom. En er þíng var sett, þá talaði Hákon konúngr, hefr þar fyrst, at þat var boð hans ok bœn við bœndr ok búþegna, ríka ok úríka, ok þarmeð við alla alþýðo, únga menn ok gamla, sælan ok vesælan, konur sem karla, at allir menn skyldo kristnast láta, ok trúa á einn guð, Krist Maríoson, en hafna blótum öllum ok heiðnom goðum, halda heilakt hinn 7da hvern dag við vinnom öllum, fasta ok hinn 7da hvern dag.

En þegar er konúngr hafði þetta uppborit fyrir alþýðo, þá varð þegar kurr mikill, kurroðo bœndr um þat, er konúngr vildi vinnur taka af þeim, ok segja at við þat mátti landit eigi byggja; en verkalýðr ok þrælar kölluðu, at þeir mætti eigi vinna, ef þeir skyldi eigi mat hafa: sögðo ok at þat var skaplöstr Hákonar konúngs, sem föður hans ok þeirra frænda, at þeir váro illir af mat sínom, þótt þeir væri mildir af gulli.

Ásbjörn af Meðalhúsom or Gaulardal stóð upp, ok svarar eyrindi konúngs ok mælti. Þat hugðo ver bœndr, Hákon konúngr! segir hann, at þá er þú hafðir et fyrsta þíng haft her í Prándheimi, ok höfðom þik til konúngs tekit, ok þegit af þer óðöl vár, at ver hefðim þá himin höndom tekit; en nú vitom ver eigi hvárt heldr er, at ver mánom frelsi þegit hafa, eða mantu nú láta þrælka oss af nýjo með undarligom hætti, at ver munim hafna átrúnaði þeim, er feðr várir hafa haft fyrir oss, ok allt forellri, fyrst um brunaöld, en nú um haugsöld, ok hafa þeir verit miklo göfgari en ver, ok hefir oss þó dugat þessi átrúnaðr. Ver höfum lagt til yðar svá mikla ástúð, at ver höfom þik ráða látit með oss öllum lögum í landino ok landsrètt. Nú er þat vili várr ok samþykki, bóndanna, at halda þau lög, sem þú settir oss her á Frostaþíngi, ok ver játaðom þer; viljom ver allir þer fylgja, ok þik til konúngs halda, meðan einnhverr er lífs bóndanna þeirra, er her ero nú á þíngino, ef þú, konúngr, vill nokkut hóf viðhafa, at beiða oss þess eins, er ver megom veita þer, ok oss se eigi ógeranda. En ef þer vilit þetta mál taka með svá mikilli freko, at deila afli ok ofríki við oss, þá höfum ver bœndr gert ráð várt, at skiljast allir við þik, ok taka oss annan höfðíngja, þann er oss haldi til þess, at ver munim í frelsi hafa þann átrúnað, sem [ver viljom. Nú skaltu, konúngr, kjósa um kosti þessa, áðr þíng se slitit.

At eyrindi þesso gerðo bœndr róm mikinn, ok segja at þeir vilja svá vera láta.

En er hljóð fèkkst, þá svarar Sigurðr jarl: Þat er vili

Hákonar konúngs, at samþykkja við yðr, bœndr, ok láta aldri skilja yðra vináttu. Bœndr segja at þeir vilja, at konúngr blóti til árs þeim ok friðar, svá sem faðir hans gerði, staðnar þá kurrinn, ok slíta þeir þíngino. Siðan talaði Sigurðr jarl við konúng, ok bað hann eigi nemast með öllu, at gera sem bœndr vildi, sagði at eigi mundi annat lýða, en sveigja til nokkot við bœndr: er þetta, konúngr, sem sjálfir þer megut heyra, vili ok ákafi höfðíngja ok þarmeð alls fólks; skolo ver, konúngr, her finna til gott ráð nokkut; ok samdist þat með þeim konúngi ok jarli.

16. Sigurðr Laða-jarl var hinn mesti blótmaðr, ok svá var Hákon fadir hans; hèlt Sigurðr jarl upp blótveizlom öllum af hendi konúngs þar í Prændalögom.

Þat var forn siðr, þá er blót skyldi vera, at allir bœndr skyldo þar koma, sem hof var, ok flytja þannug föng sín, þau er þeir skyldo hafa, meðan veizlan stóð. At veizlo þeirri skyldo allir menn öl eiga: þa var ok drepinn allskonar smali ok svá hross, en blóð þat allt, er þar kom af, þat var kallat hlaut, ok hlautbollar þat, er blóð þat stóð í, ok hlautteinar, þat var svá gert sem stöklar, með því skyldi rjóða stallana öllo saman, ok svá veggi hofsins utan ok innan, ok svá stökkva á mennina; en slátrit skyldi sjóða til mannfagnaðar. Eldar skyldo vera á miðjo gólfi í hofino, ok þar katlar yfir, ok skyldi full um eld bera. En sá er gerði veizlona, ok höfðíngi var, þá skyldi hann signa fullit ok allan blótmatinn. Skyldi fyrst Óðins full, [skyldi þat drekka til sigrs ok ríkis konúngi sínom, en síðan Njarðar full ok Freys full til árs ok friðar. Þá var mörgum mönnum títt at drekka þarnæst Braga full; menn drukko ok full frænda sinna, þeirra er göfgir höfðo verit, ok váro þat minni kölluð.

Sigurðr jarl var manna örvastr; hann gerði þat verk, er frægt var mjök, at hann gerði mikla [blótveizlo á Hlöðom, ok hèlt einn upp öllum kostnaði.

18. Um haustit at vetrnóttum var blótveizla á Löðom, ok sótti þartil konúngr. Hann hafði jafnan fyrr verit vanr, ef hann var staddr þar sem blót váro, at matast í litlu húsi með fá menn; en bœndr töldo at því, er hann sat eigi í hásæti síno, þá er mestr var mannfagnaðr; sagði jarl, at hann skyldi eigi þá svá gera, var ok svá at konúngr sat í hásæti síno. En er et fyrsta full var skenkt, þá mælti Sigurðr jarl fyrir, ok signaði Óðni, ok drakk af horninu til konúngs; konúngr tók við, ok gerði krossmark yfir: þá mælti Kárr af Grátíngi:

hví ferr konúngrinn nú svá? vill hann eigi enn blóta? Sigurðr
jarl svarar: konúngr gerir svá, sem þeir allir, er trúa á mátt
sinn ok megin, ok signa full sitt Þór; hann gerði hamarsmark
yfir, áðr hann drakk. Var þá kyrt um kveldit. Eptir um daginn, er menn gengo til borða, þá þusto bœndr at konúngi,
sögðu at þá skyldi hann eta brossaslátr; konúngr vildi þat firir
engan mun. Þá báðu þeir hann drekka soðit; hann vildi þat
eigi. Þá báðo þeir hann eta flotit; hann vildi þat ok eigi;
[ok var þá við atgöngu búit.

[Jarl kvaðst vildu sætta þá, ok bað þá hætta storminom,
ok bað hann konúng gína yfir ketilhödduna, er soðreykinn hafði
lagt upp af hrossaslátrino, ok var smjörug haddan; þá gekk
konúngr til, ok brá líndúk um hödduna, ok gein yfir, ok gekk
síðan til hásætis, ok líkaði hvárigom vel.

19. Um vetrinn eptir var búit til jólaveizlo konúngi inn
á Mœri; en er atleið jólunom, lögðo þeir stefno með ser átta
höfðingjar, er mest réðo fyrir blótum í öllum Þrændalögum;
þeir váro 4 utan or Þrándheimi: Kárr af Grýtíngi ok Ásbjörn
af Meðalhúsum, Þórbergr af Varnesi, Ormr af Ljoxu; en af
Innþrændom Bótólfr af Ölvishaugi, Narfi af Stafí Veradal, þrándr
haka af Eggjo, Þórir skegg af Húsabœ í eynni Iðri: þessir 8
menn bundust í því, at þeir fjórir af [Útþrændom skyldu eyða
kristninni, en þeir fjórir af Innþrændom skyldu neyða konúng
til blóta. Útþrændir fóro 4 skipom suðr á Mœri, ok drápo
þar presta 3, ok brenndo kirkjor 3, [fóro aptr síðan. En er
Hákon konúngr ok Sigurðr jarl komu inn á Mœri með hirð
sína, þá váro þar bœndr komnir allfjölmennt. Hinn fyrsta dag
at veizlonni [veitto bœndr, konúngi atgöngo, ok báðo hann
blóta, en hèto hánom afarkostom ella; Sigurðr jarl bar þá sátt-
mál í millom þeirra, kömr þá svá at Hákon konúngr át nok-
kura bita af hrosslifr; drakk hann þá öll minni krossalaust,
þau er bœndr skenkto hánom.

En er veizlo þessarri var lokit, fór konúngr ok jarl þegar
út á Hlaðir; var konúngr allúkátr, ok bjóst þegar í brott með
öllu liði síno or Þrándheimi, [ok mælti svá, at hann skyldi
fjölmennari koma í Þrándheim annat sinn, ok gjalda bóndom
þenna fjandskap, er þeir höfðo til hans gert. Sigurðr jarl
bað konúng gefa Þrændom þetta eigi at sök; segir svá at konúngi muni eiga þat duga at heitast eðr herja á innanlands
fólk, [þar sem mestr styrkr er landsins, sem í Þrándheimi
var. Konúngr var þá svá reiðr, at eigi mátti orðom við hann
koma; fór hann í brott or Þrándheimi, ok suðr á Mœri; dval-

dist þar um vetrinn ok um várit. En er sumraði dró hann lið at ser, ok váro þau orð á, at hann mundi fara með her þann á hendr þrændom.

20. [Hákon konúngr var þá á skip kominn, ok hafði lið mikit; þá koma hánom tíðindi sunnan or landi, þau at synir Eiríks konúngs váro komnir sunnan af Danmörk í Víkina; ok þat fylgði, at þeir höfðo elt af skipom Tryggva konúng Ólafsson austr við Sótanes; höfðo þeir þá víða herjat í Víkinni, ok höfðo margir menn undir þá gengit. En er konúngr spurði þessi tíðindi, þóttist hann liðs þurfa, sendi hann þá orð Sigurði jarli, at koma til sín, ok svá öðrum höfðíngjom, þeim er hánom var liðs at van. Sigurðr jarl kom til Hákonar konúngs, ok hafði allmikit lið; váro þar þá allir Þrændir, þeir er um vetrinn höfðo mest gengit at konúnginom, at pynda hann til blóta; váro þeir þá allir [í sætt teknir af fortölum Sigurðar jarls.

Mannjafnaðr með konúngum.

Eysteinn konúngr ok Sigurðr konúngr fóro einn vetr báðir at veizlom á Upplöndom, ok átti sín bú hvárr þeirra; en er skamt var milli þeirra bœja, er konúngar skyldo veizlor taka, þa gerðu menn þat ráð, at þeir skyldu báðir vera samt at veizlonom, ok síno sinni at hvárs búum; váro þeir fyrst báðer samt at því búi, er Eysteinn konúngr átti. En of kveldit, er menn tóku at drekka, þá var munngát ekki gott, ok váro menn hljóðer. Þá mælti Eysteinn konúngr: [Þó ero menn hljóðer! hitt er ölsiðr meiri, at menn geri ser gleði; fám oss ölteiti nökkura, man þá enn áreitast gaman manna. Sigurðr bróðir! Þat mun öllum sœmst þykkja, at við hefim nökkurar skemtunarrœður. Sigurðr konúngr svarar heldr stygt: ver þú svá málugr sem þú vill, en lát mik ná at þegja fyrir þer!

Eysteinn konúngr mælti: sá ölsiðr hefir opt verit, at menn taka ser jafnaðarmenn, vil ek her svá vera láta. Þá þagðe Sigurðr konúngr.

Se ek, segir Eysteinn konúngr, at [ek verð at hefja þessa teiti; mun ek taka þik, bróðer! til jafnaðarmanns mer: fœri ek þat til, at jafnt nafn höfom við báðer, ok jafna eign, geri ek ok engi mun ættar okkarrar eða uppfœzlu.

Þá svarar Sigurðr konúngr: mantu þat eigi, er ek braut þik á bak, ef ek vilda, ok vartu vetri ellri!

Eysteinn konúngr svaraði: eigi man ek hitt siðr, er þu fèkkt ekki leikit, þat er mjúkleikr var í.

Þá mælti Sigurðr konúngr: mantu hversu of sundet fór með okkr? ek mátta kefja þik, ef ek vilda!

Eysteinn sagði: ekki svam ek skemra en þú, ok eigi var ek verr kafsyndr; ek kunna ok á ísleggjom, svá at engan vissa ek, þann [er kepðe við mik, en þú kunnir þat eigi heldr en naut.

Sigurðr konúngr svarar: höfðíngligri iðrótt ok nytsamligri þykki mer sú, at kunna vel við boga; ætla ek at þú nýtir eigi boga minn, þótto spyrnir fótom í.

Eysteinn segir: ekki em ek bogsterkr svá sem þú, en minna mun skilja beinskeyti okkra, ok myklo kann ek betr en þú á skíðom, ok hafðe þat enn [verit kallat fyrr góð iðrótt.

Sigurðr segir: þess þykkir mikill munr, at þat er höfðíngligra, at sá er yfirmaðr skal vera annarra manna, se mikill í flokki, sterkr ok vápnfœrr betr en aðrir, auðsær ok auðkendr, þá er [margir eru saman.

Eysteinn segir: eigi er þat síðr einkanna hlutr, at maðr se fríðr sánom, ok er sá ok auðkendr í mannfjölda, þikki mer þat ok höfðingligt, þvíat fíiðleikinom samir hinn bezti búnaðr. Kann ek ok myklo betr til laga en þú; ok svá, hvat sem við skolum tala, em ek myklo slèttorðari.

Sigurðr svarar: Vera kann at þú hafir numit fleiri lögpretto, þvíat ek átta þá annat at starfa; ok engi frýr þer slèttmælis, en hitt mæla margir, at þú ser ekki allfastorðr, ok lítið mark se hverjo þú heitr, ok mælir eptir þeim er þá ero hjá, ok er þat ekki konúnglikt.

Eysteinn svarar: þat herr til þess, er menn bera mál sín fyrir mik, þá hugsa ek þat fyrst, at lúka svá hvers manns máli, at þeim mætti bezt þykkja; þá kemr opt annarr, sá er mál á við hann, verðr þá jafnan dregit til ok miðlat, svá at báðom skyldi líka. Hitt er ok, at ek heit því er ek em beðenn, þvíat ek vilda, at allir fœri fegnir af mínom funde; se ek hinn kost, ef ek vil hafa sem þú gerir, at heita öllum illu, en engi heyri ek efndanna frýja.

Sigurðr svarar: þat hefir verit mál manna, at ferð sú er ek fór or lande væri heldr höfðínglig, en þú sazt heima meðan, sem dóttir föður þíns.

Eysteinn svarar: nú greiptu á kýlino! eigi mynda ek þessa rœðo vekja, ef ek kynna her engu [um at svara: nær þótti

mer hino, at ek gerða þik heiman sem systor mína, aðr þú
yrðir búinn til fararinnar.

Sigurðr svarar: heyrt muntu þat hafa, at ek átta orrostor
margar í Serklandi, ok fèkk í öllum sigr, ok margskonar gjör-
simar, þær er eigi hafa slíkar komit híngat í land; þótta ek
þar mest verðr, er ek fann göfgasta menn, en ek hygg, at
eigi hafir þú enn [hleypt heimdreganom. Fór ek til Jórsala,
segir hann, ok kom ek við Púl, ok sá ek þig eigi þar, bróðir!
Ek gaf konúngdóm Rodgeiri jarli hínom ríka; vann ek átta
orrostor, ok vartu at aungarri. Fór ek til grafar drottins, ok
sá ek þig eigi þar, bróðir! Fór ek í ána Jórdán, þar sem
drottinn [var skírðr í, ok svam ek út yfir ána, ok sá ek þig
eigi þar, [en út á bakkanom var kjarr nökkut', ok knýtta ek
þer þar knút á kjarrino, ok bíðr þín þar; [ok mælta ek svá
fyrir, at þú skylder leysa, bróðer! eða hafa ellar þvílíkan for-
mála, sem þar var álagðr.

Þá mælti Eysteinn konúngr: smátt mun ek hafa hérímóti:
Norðr í Vágom setta ek fiskimannabúðir, at fátœkir menn mætti
nærast til lífshjálpar, ok setta ek þar prestvist, ok lagða ek fe
til kirkju þeirrar, er náliga var allt heiðit áðr; máno þeír
menn muna, at Eysteinn konúngr hefir verit í Noregi. Um
Dofra fjall var för or Þrándheimi; urðo menn þar jafnan úti,
ok fóro þar margir menn hörðom förum, lèt ek þar sælohús
gera, ok fe tilleggja, ok munu þeir vita, at Eysteinn konúngr
hefir verit í Noregi. Fyrir Agðanesi voru öræfi ok hafnleysi,
fórust mörg skip; þar er nú höfn ger ok gott skipalægi, ok
kirkja gjör. Síðan lèt ek vita gera á háfjöllom; nú munu þessa
njóta allir menn innanlands. Höllina lèt ek gera í Björgyn
ok postulakirkju ok rið milli; munu konúngar þeir muna nafn
mitt, er eptir koma. Mikjalskirkju lèt ek gera ok múnklifi;
skipaða et ok lögonom, bróðir, at hverr mætti hafa rèttindi við
annan, ok ef þau ero haldin, þá mun betr fara landsstjórnin.
Stöpulinn lèt ek gera í Sinhólmssundi. Þeim jamtom höfom
ver ok snúit undir þetta ríki, meir með bliðom orðom ok viti
en með ágáng eðr ófriði. Nú er þetta smátt at telja, en égi
veit ek víst at landsbúunom se þetta óhallkvæmara, en þótt
þú brytjaðir blámenn fyrir fjandann [á Serklandi, ok hrapa
þeim svá til helvítis. En þar sem þú hrósaðir góðgerníngom
þínom, ætla ek mer eigi minna til sálubótar staði þá, er ek
lèt setja hreinlífismönnum. En þar sem þú reitt mer knútinn,
ok mun ek þann eigi leysa, en ríða mátta ek þer þann knút,
[ef ek vilda, at þú værir aldregi konúngr í Noregi, þá er þú

sigldir einskipa í her minn, er þú komt í land. Líti nú vittrir menn hvat þú hefir umfram, ok vita skulut þer þat, gullháls-arnir, at menn muno enn jafnast við iðr í Noregi. Eptir þat þögnuðo þeir baðer, ok var hvártveggi reiðr. Fleiri lutir urðo þeir í skiptom þeirra brœðra, er þat fanst, at hvárr dró sik fram ok sitt mál, ok vildi vera öðrom meiri, en þó hèlzt friðr [millum þeirra, meðan þeir lifðo.

Af Njálssaga.

Gunnarr á Hlíðarenda.

19... Gunnarr Hámundarson bjó at Hlíðarenda í Fljóts-hlíð; hann var mikill maðr vexti ok sterkr, [manna bezt vígr: hann hjó báðum höndum ok skaut, ef hann vildi, ok hann vá svá skjótt með sverði¹, at þrjú þóttu á lopti at sjá; hann skaut manna bezt af boga, ok hœfði allt þat er hann skaut til; hann hljóp meir en bæð sína með öllum herklæðum, ok eigi skemra aptr en fram fyrir sik; hann var syndr sem selr; ok eigi var sá leikr, er nokkurr þyrfti við hann at keppa; ok hefir svá verit sagt, at eingi væri hans jafníngi. Hann var vænn at yfirlitum ok ljós-litaðr, rètt-nefjaðr ok hafit upp í fra-manvert, bláeygr ok snareygr, ok roði í kinnunum, hárit mikit, ok fór vel ok vel litt; manna kurteisastr var hann, harðgjörr í öllu, femildr ok stiltr vel, vinfastr ok vinavandr; hann var vel auðigr at fe; bróðir hans hèt Kolskeggr, hann var mikill maðr ok sterkr, drengr góðr ok öruggr í öllu. Annarr bróðir hans hèt Hjörtr, hann var þá í bernsku...

20... Njáll bjó at Bergþórshváli í Landeyjum, annat bú átti hann í Þórólfsfelli. Njáll var vel auðigr at fe ok vænn at áliti, hánom vox eigi skegg. Hann var lögmaðr svá mikill, at eingi fannst hans jafníngi; vitr var hann ok forspár, heil-ráðr ok góðgjarn, ok varð allt at ráði, þat er hann rèð mön-num, hógværr ok drenglyndr; hann leysti hvers manns vandræði, er á hans fund kom. Bergþóra hèt kona hans, hon var Skar-pheðins dóttir, kvennskörúngr mikill ok drengr góðr, ok nokkut skaphörð; þau áttu 6 börn, dœtr þrjár ok sonu þrjá, ok koma þeir allir við þessa sögu síðan.

25... Nú skal nefna sonu Njáls: Skarpheðinn hèt hinn

elzti, hann var mikill maðr vexti ok styrkr, vel vígr, syndr
sem slr, manna fóthvatastr, ok skjótr ok öruggr, gagnorðr ok
skjótorðr, ok skáld gott, en þó laungum vel stiltr; hann var
jarpr á hár, ok sveipr í hárinu, augðr vel, fölleitr ok skarpleitr,
liðr á nefi, ok lá hátt tanngarðrinn, munnljótr mjök, ok þó
manna hermannligstr. Grímr hèt annarr son Njáls, hann var
fríðr sánum, ok hærðr vel, dökkr á hár, ok fríðari sánum en
Skarpheðinn, mikill ok sterkr. Helgi hèt inn þriði son Njáls,
hann var friðr sýnum ok hærðr vel, hann var styrkr maðr ok
vígr vel, hann var vitr maðr ok stiltr vel; allir váru þeir ók-
vángaðir synir Njáls. Höskuldr hèt hinn fjórði son Njáls, hann
var laungetinn, móðir hans var Hróðný, ok var Höskulds dóttir,
systir Íngjalds frá Keldum.

33. Gunnarr reið ok þeir allir, en er þeir komu á þíng,
þá váru þeir svá vel búnir, at öngir voru þar jafnvel búnir,
ok fóru menn út or hverri búð at undrast þá. Gunnarr reið
til búðar Rángæínga, ok var þar með frændum sínum. Margir menn fóru at finna Gunnarr, ok spyrja hann tíðinda; hann
var við alla menn lèttr ok kátr, ok sagði öllum slíkt er vildu.

Þat var einn dag, er Gunnarr gekk frá lögbergi, hann
gekk fyrir mosfellíngabúð, þá sá hann kono fara í móti ser,
ok var vel búin, en er þau fundust, kvaddi hon þegar Gunnar,
hann tók vel kveðju hennar, ok spyrr hvat kvenna hon væri.
Hon nefndist Hallgerðr, ok kvaðst vera dóttir Höskulds Dala-
akollssonar; hon mælti til hans djarfliga, ok bað segja ser frá
ferðum sínum, en hann kvaðst ekki varna mundu henni máls;
settust þau þá niðr, ok töluðu. Hon var svá búin, at hon var
í rauðu kyltli, ok hafði yfir ser skallazskikkju [blaðbúna í skaut
niðr; hárit tók ofan á bríngu henni, ok var bæði mikit ok
fagrt. Gunnarr var í skallazklæðum, er Haraldr konúngr Gormsson gaf hánum; hann hafði ok gullhríng á hendi, þann er
Hákon jarl gaf hánum.

Þau töluðu lengi hátt, þar kom er hann spurði, hvárt
hon væri ógefin. Hon sagði at svá væri: ok er þat [ekki
margra at hætta á þat. Þikki þer hvergi fullkosta? Eigi er
þat, segir hon, en mannvönd mun ek vera. Hversu munt þú
svara, ef ek bið þín? Þat man þer ekki í hug, segir hon.
Eigi er þat, segir hann. Ef þer er nokkurr hugr á, þá finn
þú föður minn. Síðan skildu þau talit.

Gunnarr gekk þegar til búðar Dalamanna, ok fann mann
úti fyrir búðinni, ok spyrr hvárt Höskuldr væri í búð; sá segir
at hann væri í búð; gekk þá Gunnarr inn. Höskuldr ok Rútr

tóku vel við Gunnari, hann settist niðr á meðal þeirra, ok fannst þat ekki í tali þeirra, at þar hefði missætti verit í meðal. Þar kom niðr rœða Gunnars, hversu þeir brœðr mundu því svara, ef hann bæði Hallgerðar. Vel segir Höskuldr, ef þer er þat alugat. Gunnarr segir ser þat alvöru: en svá skildu ver næstum, at mörgum mundi þat þikkja líkligt, at her mundi ekki samband verða. Hversu lízt þer, Rútr frændi? segir Höskuldr. Rútr svaraði: ekki þikki mer þetta jafnræði. Hvat finnr þú til þess? segir Gunnarr. Rútr mælti: því mun ek svara þer um þetta, er satt er; þú ert maðr vaskr, ok vel at þer, en hon er blandin mjök, ok vil ek þik í öngu svíkja. Vel man þer fara, segir Gunnarr, en þó mun ek þat fyrir satt hafa, at þer virðit í fornan fjandskap, ef þer vilit eigi gera mer kostinn. Eigi er þat, segir Rútr; meir er hitt, at ek se at þú mátt nú ekki viðgera; en þótt ver kaupim eigi, þá vildim ver þó vera vinir þínir. Ek hefi talat við hana, segir Gunnarr, ok er þat ekki fjarri hennar skapi. Rútr mælti: veit ek at báðum er þetta girnda ráð, hættit þit ok mestu til, hversu ferr.

Rútr sagði Gunnari ófregit allt um skapferði Hallgerðar, ok þótti Gunnari fyrst œrit mart, þat er áfátt var, en þar kom síðar, at saman dró kaupmála með þeim. Var þá sent eptir Hallgerði, var þá talat um málit, svá at hon var við. Lètu þeir nú sem fyrr, at hon festi sik sjálf; skyldi þetta boð vera at Hlíðarenda, ok skyldi fara fyrst leyniliga, en þó kom þar, er allir vissu.

Gunnarr reið heim af þíngi, ok kom til Bergþórshvols, ok sagði Njáli frá kaupum sínum; hann tók þessu þúngliga. Gunnarr spyrr hví Njáli þótti þetta svá úráðligt? Þvíat af henni man standast allt it illa, er hon kemr austr híngat, segir Njáll. Aldri skal hon spilla okkru vinfengi, segir Gunnarr. Þat man þó [svá nær fara, segir Njáll, en þó mant þú jafnan bœta fyrir henni. Gunnarr bauð Njáli til boðs ok öllum þeim þaðan, sem hann vildi at fœri. Njáll hèt at fara. Síðan reið Gunnarr heim, ok reið um heraðit, at bjóða mönnum.

PART IV.

Modern Icelandic.

This part has been added for Travellers and for practical purposes; and will, it is hoped, be a welcome assistant for travellers in Iceland.

The Modern Orthography and Grammar is the same as the ancient, except *k*, which is in modern orthography frequently changed into the softer *g*, and *t*, which is frequently changed into ð.

Modern Icelandic.

For Travellers.

1. Alphabetical Vocabulary.

accept	ganga að	*afternoon*	síðari hluti
acceptable	aðgengilegur		dags.
accommodate	útvega	*again*	aptur
can you accommodate me	getið þér útvegað mér	*age*	aldur
		agent	umboðsmaður
account	reikningur	*air*	lopt
give me my account	gefið mer reikninginn minn	*ale*	öl
		a glass of ale	glas af öli
I admire	eg dáist að	*all*	allur
advice	ráð	*not at all*	alls eigi
give me your advice	gefið mér yðar ráð	*nothing at all*	alls ekkert
		alone	einn, aleinn
after	eptir	*also*	líka

altogether	allir saman, alveg	bath	bað	
always	alltaf	I want a bath	eg vil fá bað	
and	og	to be	að vera	
angler	önglari	be quick	verið fljótur	
animal	dýr	let it be	látið það vera	
to answer	að svara			
answer me please	Gjörið svo vel að svara mér	because	af þvíað	
answer slowly	svarið seint	bed	rúm	
apartment	herbergi	give me a bed	látið mig fá rúm	
have you an apartment to let?	hafið þér herbergi til leigu?	I go to bed	eg fer að hátta	
apple	epli	beef	nautakjöt	
the arm	handleggurinn	roast beef beef steakes	{ nautakjöts-steik	
to arrive	að koma	beer	bjór	
to ascend	að fara uppá	I want some beer	eg vil fá bjór	
I want to ascend the mountain	eg vil fara uppá fjallið	to beg	að biðja	
to ask	að spyrja, biðja	I beg of you	eg bið yður	
ask him	spyrjið hann	behind	eptir	
to assist	að hjálpa	I left it behind	eg skildi það eptir	
assist me	hjálpið mér	the bell	bjallan, klukkan	
at	í, á	the bill	reikningurinn	
at home	heima	to bind	að binda	
at sea	á sjó	bind it up	bindið það upp	
not at all	alls eigi	the bird	fuglinn	
attendant	þénari	can you tell me where to get board and lodgings	Getið þér sagt mér, hvar má fá kost og húsnæði?	
I want an attendant	eg vil fá þénara			
back	aptur	boat	bátur	
let us go back	förum aptur, snúum aptur	book	bók	
bacon	flesk	bookseller	bókasölumaður	
bad	vondur	boot	stigvél	
bandage	umbúðir	I want my boots mended	eg þarf að fá gjört vid stígvélin mín	
bank	banki			
bank note	bankaseðill	brush my boots	burstaðu stígvélin mín	
banker	víxlari			
the barber	rakarinn			

boot jack	stigvéla togari	candle	kerti
box	askja, kassi	I wanta	eg þarf kerti
brandy	brennivín, ko-	candle	
	níakk	care	umhyggja, vari
I want some	egvil fá brenn-	take care	takid vara
brandy	ivín	carriage	vagn
fill my flask	fyllið flöskuna	to carry	að bera
with brandy	mína með	carry this	berið þetta
	brennivíni	cartridge	skotmanns ves-
bread	brauð		ki
breakfast	morgunverður	cattle	nautpeningur
I want to	eg vil fá mor-	certain	viss
breakfast	gunverð	chair	stóll
bridge	brú	chamber pot	náttpottur
bring	bera, færa	change	skipti
bring me	færið mér	give me change	gefið mér
bring me some	færið mér		skipti
	nokkuð	to charge	að setja upp,
a brush	bursti		heimta
brush my	burstið fötin	what do you	hvað setið þér
clothes	mín	charge	upp?
but	en	cheap	ódýr
butter	smjör	cheese	ostur
to buy	að kaupa	chest	kista
by	hjá, með, af	- of drawers	dragkista
by and by	við og við, bráð-	chicken	hænuungi,
	um		kjúklingur
by all means	fyrir alla muni	child	barn
by no means	fyrir engan	church	kirkja
	mun, engan	chymist	efnafræðingur
	veginn	cigar	vindill
cabbage	kál	city	bær, staður
cabbin	káhetta	clean	hreinn
to call	að kalla	cloak	kápa
call the wai-	kallið á þjón-	clock	klukka
ter	inn	closet	afhús
call the man	kallið á mann-	coach	vagn
	inn	coat	frakki
what do you	hvað kallið	coffee	kaffi
call that?	þér það?	give me some	gefið mér
can	að geta, eg get	coffee	kaffi
can you	getið þér?	coffee-house	kaffihús

cold	kaldur
I feel very cold	mér er mjög kalt
comb	kambur
to come	að koma
come here	komið hér
come with me	komið með mér
a conveyance	flutningur
to cook	að elda
cost	kosta
what does it cost?	hvað kostar það
country	land
courier	hraðsendiboði
cow	kýr
cream	rjómi
give me some cream	gefið mér rjóma
cup	bolli
cup and saucer	bolli og undirskál
to cut	að skera
cut it	að skera það
damp	rakur, votur
I hope the sheets are not damp	eg vona, að rekkvoðirnar sé ekki rakar
danish	danska
do you speak danish	talið þér dönsku?
what is that called in danish	hvað er það kallad á dönsku?
I do not speak danish	eg tala ekki dönsku
I understand a little danish	eg skil dálitið í dönsku
dark	dimmur
day	dagur
to-day	í dag

at day break	í dögun
dear	dýr
this is very dear	þetta er mjög dýrt
delightful	yndislegur
dentist	tannlæknir
departure	burtför
descend	fara niður
let us descend	förum niður
dialect	mállýzka
what dialect do they speak here?	hvaða mállýzku tala þeir hér?
difficult	örðugur
dinner	miðdagsverður
I want to dine	eg vil fá miðdagsverð
distance	fjarlægð, vegalengd
what is the distance?	hvað er vegalengdin?
to do	að gjöra
do this	gjörið þetta
do that	gjörið hitt
do it	gjörið það
do me	gjörið fyrir mig
dont do it.	gjörið það ekki
the doctor	læknirinn
dog	hundur
door	dyr
to. doubt	að efa
I doubt it	eg efa það
down	niður
let us go down	förum niður
drawers	nærbuxur
to dress	að klœða sig
to drink	að drekka
I want to drink	eg vil fá að drekka
dry	þur
each	hver
eagle	örn

early	snemma	field	engi
earth	jörð	finger	fingur
east	austur	fire	eldur
east wind	austanvindur	let us make	kveykjum upp
easy	auðveldur, hæ-gur	a fire	eld
to eat	að eta, borða	I want some fire	eg vil fá eld
I want to eat	eg vil fá að borða	a fish	fiskur
let us eat	látum oss borða	to fish	að fiska
		let us catch a fish	látum oss veiða fisk
have you anything to eat?	hafið þér nokk-uð að borða?	my fishing rod	fiskistöngin mín
		flask	flaska, púður-horn
egg	egg	fog	þoka
give me two eggs	gefið mér tvö egg	foot	fótur
to engage	að festa	my foot is sore	fóturinn á mér er viðkvœmur
engage a guide	festa fylgdar-mann	for	þvíað
enough	nóg	fork	gaffall
evening	kvöld	free	frjáls
every	sérhver	fruit	ávöxtur
every day	sérhvern dag	full	fullur
eye	auga	game	veiði
my eye pains	mér er illt í auganu	its there any game here?	er nokkur-veiði hér
face	andlit	german	þýzkur
far	langt	to get	að fá, útvega
is it far from here?	er það langt héðan?	get me	útvegið mér
		get it	útvegið það
how far is it from here?	hvað langt er það héðan?	gin	einirberja-brennivín
a farm	bær	to give	að gefa
fast	fljótt	give me	gefið mér
go faster	gangið fljótar	give it	gefið það
do not speak so fast	talið ekki svona fljótt	a glass	glas
		to go	að ganga, fara, koma
faster	fljótar		
fellow	maður	go with me	komið með mér
you are a good fellow	þér eruð góð-ur maður	go away	farið í burtu

go back	farið aptur	head	höfuð
go down	farið niður	to hear	að heyra
go up	farið upp	do you hear?	heyriðþér
good	góður	heart	hjarta
very good	mikið góður	heat	hiti
better	betri	great heat	mikill hiti
best	beztur	heavy	þungur
be so good	verið svo góð-ur	height	hæð
have the good-ness	gjörið svo vel	what is the height	hvað er hæðin?
great	mikill	help	hjálp
a great deal	mikill hluti	help me	hjálpið mér
gun	byssa	give me a help	veitið mér hjálp
give me my gun	fáið mér bys-suna mína	hen	hæna
where is my gun?	hvar er byssan mín?	here	hér
		come here	komið hér
powder	púður	high	hár
		how high is it?	hvað hátt er það?
hair	hár	hill	hæð
hair brush	hárbursti	to hire	að leigja
half	hálfur	to hold	að halda
ham	hangið svíns-læri	hold this	haldið á þessu
		home	heimili
hand	hönd	is this your home?	er þetta yðar heimili?
give me your hand	gefið mér hönd yðar að	honest	ráðvandur
hand it me	réttið mér þ	I want an ho-nest fellow	eg vil fá ráð-vandan mann
handkerchief	vasaklútur	horse	hestur
handsome	fallegur	horseshoe	skeifa
harbour	höfn	hot	heitur
hard	harður	it is very hot	það er mikið heitt
hare	héri		
harness	aktygi	I want it hot	eg vil fá það heitt
hat	hattur		
hatbox	hattaskja	hotel	gestgjafahús
to have	að hafa	hour	klukkustund
have you?	hafið þér	house	hús
let me have.	látið mig hafa	how	hversu
hay	hey	how much	hversu mikið
he	hann		

hunger	hungur	do you know	vitið þér
hungry	hungraður	lake	vatn
I am hungry	eg er hung-	lamp	lampi
	raður	land	land
a hut	kofi	landlord	húsbóndi
Ice	ís	language	tunga
Iceland	Ísland	Lapland	Lappland
an Icelander	Íslendingur	late	seint
are you an	eruð þér Ís-	it is very late	það er mjög
Icelander?	lendingur?	lava	seint hraun
do you speak	talið þér ís-	to lay	að leggja
Icelandic?	lenzku?	lay it down	leggið það-
what do you	hvað kallið þér		niður
call this in	þetta á ís-	lay down	leggið niður
icelandic?	lenzku?	to lead	að leiða, liggja
if	ef	does the way	liggur vegur-
ill	illt	lead up?	inn upp?
I feel ill	} mér er illt	lead to right	leiða á réttan
I am ill		way	veg
fetch a doctor	sækið læknir	left	vinstri
in	í, á	to the left	til vinstri
in the city	í bænum	to let	að láta
in the country	á landinu	let me alone	látið mig vera
indeed	svo! sannarlega	let it be	látið það vera
the inn	veitingahús	let me do it	látið mig gjöra
inn keeper	veitingamaður		það
ink	blek	let it be done	látið það vera
insect	skorkvikindi		gjört
iron	járn	letter	bréf
island	ey	any letters for	nokkur bréf
it	það	me?	til mín?
to keep	geyma	send the letter	sendið bréfið
keep it for me	geymið það	to the Post	á póst húsið
	fyrir mig	life	líf
key	lykill	the light	ljósið
knife	hnífur	bring a light	komið með
give me a	ljáið mér hníf		ljós
knife		strike a light	kveikið ljós
where is my	hvar er hníf-	light the candle	kveikið á kert-
knife?	urinn minn		inu
to know	að vita, þekkja	like	líka, þykja
I know	eg veit		vænt um

I should like	mér skyldi þykja vænt um
linnen	línföt
wash my linnen	þvoið línfötin mín
I want my linnen washed immediately	eg þarf að fá línfötin mín þvegin undireins
little	lítill
to live	að lifa
liver	lifur
loaf	brauð
lock	lás, skrá
lock the door	læsið dyrunum
lodging	leiguherbergi
long	langur, lengi
to look	að líta
looking glass	spegill
to lose	að missa, tína
I have lost	eg hefi misst
have you lost?	hafið þér misst
luggage	farangur
where is my luggage?	hvar er farangurinn minn?
to make	að gjöra
make haste	flýtið yður
man	maður
many	margur
market	markaður
me	mig, mér
meat	kjöt
roast meat	steikt kjöt
boiled meat	soðið kjöt
to meet	að mæta
meet me	mætið mér
merchant	kaupmaður
milk	mjólk
have you any milk?	hafið þér nokkra mjólk

give me some milk	gefið mér mjólk
mill	mynla
money	peningar
moon	máni, tungl
moor	mýri
more	meira
more and more	meira og meira
most	mest
morning	morgun
mother	móðir
much	mikið
it is too much	það er of mikið
much more	mikið meira
so much	svo mikið
must. v. aux.	verða, hljóta
you must do it	þér verðið að gjöra það
mustard	mustarður
mutton	sauðakjöt
my	minn
nail	nögl
name	nafn
what is your name?	hvað er nafn yðar?
my name is N.	nafn mitt er N
narrow	þröngur
nasty	slæmur
near	nærri
it is near?	er það nærri?
necessary	nauðsynlegur
needle	nál
neither	hvorki
neither-nor	hvorki-né
never	aldrei
new	nýr
news	tíðindi
next	næst
night	nótt
last night	í gærkvöldi
no	enginn

no one	enginn	*pear*	pera
nobody	enginn maður	*pen*	penni
n r	norður	*penknife*	pennahnífur
north wind	norðan vindur	*pencil*	ritblý
not	ekki	*people*	lýður
not yet	ekki enn þá	*pepper*	pipar
now	nú	*perhaps*	ef til vill
oats	hafrar	*person*	maður
to oblige	hjálpa um	*a pin*	títuprjónn
oblige me	hjálpið mér um	*pipe*	pípa
		pistol	smábyssa
ocean	haf	*place*	staður
off	burtu	*plate*	diskur
far off	langt í burtu	*poor*	fátækur, vesall
often	opt	*pork*	svínakjöt
oil	olía, lýsi	*porter*	burðarmaður
old	gamall	*portmanteau*	ferðataska
omlet	eggjakaka	*post*	póstur
on	á	*where is the post office?*	hvar er póst-skrifstofan?
only	einungis		
open	opinn	*postage*	burðareyrir
or	eða	*potatoe*	jarðepli, kart-apla
an orange	apelsína		
other	annarr	*powder*	púður
the other man	hinn maðurinn	*pronounce*	bera fram
the other day	um daginn	*pronounce this to me*	berið þér þetta fram fyrir mig
each other	hver annan		
out	út	*provisions*	matvæli, nesti
out of	út úr	*to put*	að setja
over	yfir	*put it down*	setið það niður
ox	uxi	*put it there*	setið það þarna
to pack	að láta uppá		
the mules	úlfaldarnir	*quick*	fljótur
paper	pappír	*railway*	járnbraut
to pay	að borga	*rain*	regn
I want to pay	eg ætla að borga?	*rain water*	regnvatn
what have I to pay?	hvað á eg að borga	*it is a rainy day*	það er rigningar dagur í dag
peak	tindur	*rainy*	regnlegur
can we ascent the peak?	getum við farið uppá tindinn	*will it rain?*	ætlar hann að rigna?

raw	hrár
to read	að lesa
read it to me	lesið það fyrir mig
ready	tilbúinn
is every thing ready?	er allt tilbúið?
are you ready?	eruð þér tilbúinn
rest	hvíld
let us rest here	við skulum hvíla hérna
to return	að fara aptur
rich	ríkur
ride	ríða
I will ride	eg vil ríða
rifle	kúlubyssa
right	réttur
is this right?	er þetta rétt
is it the right way?	er þetta sá rétti vegur?
to the right	til hægri
ripe	þroskaður
river	á
road	vegur
the high road	alfaravegur
rough	ósléttur
a rough road	ósléttur vegur
rum	romm
to run	að hlaupa
saddle	hnakkur, söðull
saddlebags	hnakkpoki
horse	hestur
salt	salt
have you any salt?	hafið þér nokkuð salt?
sand	sandur
to say	að segja
the sea	sjórinn
the sea bird	sjófuglinn
the sea shore	sjáfarströndin
to see	að sjá

let us see	látum oss sjá
to send	að senda
send it away	sendið það í burtu
servant	þjónn
to set	að setja
set it down	setið það niður
to sew	að sauma
to shave	að raka
she	hún
ship	skip
shirt	skirta
shoe	skór
shoemaker	skóari
sick	sjúkur
to sit	að sitja
to sleep	að sofa
sleep	svefn
slow	seinn
small	lítill
to smoak	að reykja
soap	sápa
soon	bráðum
speak	tala
do you speak english?	talið þér ensku?
or french	eða frakknesku
or icelandic	eða íslenzku
or danish?	eða dönsku?
I do not speak	eg tala ekki
I speak a little	eg tala dálítið
speak slowly	talið hægt
spoon	skeið, spónn
steamer	gufuskip
steel	stál
stocking	sokkur
stone	steinn
straw	strá
street	stræti
strong	sterkur
stupid	heimskur

sugar	sikur	towel	handklæði
sun	sól	town	bær, staður
supper	kvöldverður	travel	ferð
sweet	sætur	trowsers	buxur
to swim	að synda	true	sannur
table	borð	trunk	koffort
the tailor	skraddarinn	under	undir
to take	að taka	understand	skilja
take me	takið mig	do you under-	skilið þér mig?
take it	takið það	stand me?	
tea	tevatn	I do not un-	eg skil yður
a cup of tea	tevatnsbolli	derstand you	ekki
have you any	hafið þér nokk-	can you un-	getið þér
tea	uð tevatn	derstand?	skilið?
hot tea	heitt tevatn	not much	ekki mikið
cold tea	kalt tevatn	only a little	einungis dálít-
tea spoon	teskeið		ið
to tell	að segja	until	til
tell me	segið mér	up	upp
I tell you	eg segi yður	up the hill	upp hæðina
tent	tjald	up the stream	upp eptir fljót-
thanks	þakkir		inu
many thanks	margfaldar	upon	á
	þakkir	vegetables	kálmeti
I thank you	eg þakka yður	very	mjög
that	að	the waiter	þjónninn
theatre	leikhús	to walk	að ganga
then	þá	warm	heitur
there	þar	to wash	að þvo
thick	þykkur	the washing	þvotturinn
thin	þunnur	the watch	úrið
thirsty	þyrstur	water	vatn
I am very	eg er mikið	give me some	gefið mér vatn
thirsty	þyrstur	water	
this	þessi	the water closet	náðhúsið
time	tími	the way	vegurinn
what is the	hvað er fram-	show me the	vísið mér veg-
time?	orðið?	way	inn
to	til, í, á	which way	hvaða veg verð
to-day	í dag	must I go?	eg að fara?
to-morrow	á morgun	which is the	hvar er vegur-
tobacco	tóbak	way to?	inn til?

we -	vér, við	window	gluggi
weather	veður	wine	vín
will it be fair weather?	ætli það verði gott veður	have you any wine?	hafið þér nokkuð vín
will it be bad weather?	ætli það verði vont veður	Portwine or Sherry?	portvín eða sérrí
well	gott, góður, frískur	with	með
		without	án
I am not well	eg er ekki góður, frískur	woman	kona
		wood	skógur, viður
west	vestur	to write	að skrifa
wet	votur	to write a letter	að skrifa bréf
what	hvað		
where	hvar	year	ár
when	hvenær	yes	já
which	hver, hvaða	yet	enn, ennþá
why?	því	you	þér
will you	vilið þér	you are	þér eruð
wild	viltur	are you?	eruð þér?
wind	vindur	yourself	þér sjálfur

11. Necessary Questions.

I want	Mig vantar, eg þarf, eg vil fá	some brandy	brennivín, koníakk
some bacon	flesk	a bottle of brandy	brennivíns flösku
a banker	víxlara	some bread	brauð
a bath	bað	to breakfast	að borða morgunverð
my beard shaved	skegg mitt rakað	tea, coffee,	tevatn, kaffi
a bedroom	svefnherbergi	two eggs and bacon	tvö egg og flesk
some beer	bjór	or ham	eða hangið svínslæri
my bill	reikninginn minn	a brush	bursta
the bill of fare	matarlistann	some butter	smjör
my boots cleaned	stígvélin mín hreinsuð	to buy	að kaupa
my boots soled	stígvélin mín sóluð	my carpetbag	ferðapokann minn
		a carriage	vagn

Icelandic Grammar.

8

for one, two hours	eina, tvær stundir	a horse	hest
for a day	einn dag	some ink	blek
the chamber-maid	þjónustu stúlku	an interpreter	túlk
		the landlord	húsbóndann
some cheese	ost	my letters	bréfin mín
to change some money	að skipta nokkrum peningum	to write a letter	að skrifa bréf
		to post a letter	að koma bréfi á póstlinn
my coat	frakkann minn	my linnen washed	línfötin mín þvegin
my collars washed	kragana mína þvegna	my baggage	farangurinn minn
a cup of coffee	kaffibolla	some meat	kjöt
a cup of tea	tevatnsbolla	cold meat	kalt kjöt
a comb	kamb	hot meat	heitt kjöt
to dine	að borða miðdagsverð	pepper	pipar
		pens	penna
fish	fisk	the porter	burðarmanninn
roast meat	steikt kjöt	roast beaf	steikt nautakjöt
boiled meat	soðið kjöt	mutton	- sauðakjöt
potatoes	jarðepli, kartöplur	veal	- kálfskjöt
		pork	- svínakjöt
vegetables	kálmeti	the railway	járnbrautin
pudding	búðing	a room	herbergi
salad	salat	some salt	salt
drawers	nærbuxur	to see the town	að sjá bæinn
eggs	egg	- - - theatre	- - leikhúsið
a fire	eld		
to get up at 5 o'clock	að fara á fætur klukkan fimm	to see the promenade	- - skemmtigöngusviðið
a glass of water	glas af vatni	dry sheets	þurrar rekkvoðir
a glass of wine	glas af víni		
to go to the ..	að fara til	shirts	skirtur
to go by steamer	að fara med gufuskipi	my shirts washed	skirturnar mínar þvegnar
to go by railway	að fara með járnbraut	a sitting room	herbergi
		my slippers	morgunskóna mína
to go to bed	að hátta		
some ham	hangið svínslæri	some soap	sápu
		a stick	staf
a good hotel	gott gestgjafahús	my stockings	sokkana mína
		suggar	sikur

supper	kvöldverð	help me	hjálpa mér
a ticket	bílæti	let me	láta mig
for the 1st class	á fyrsta pláss	let me have	láta mig hafa
for the 2nd class	á annað pláss	look for	gá að
toothbrush	tannbursta	look after	líta eptir
my trowsers	buxurnar mínar	make	gjöra
my trunk	koffortið mitt	mend	gjöra við
umbrella	regnhlíf	oblige	hjálpa um
you to wake me	að þér vekið	pick	tína
at . . .	mig um . . .	please	þóknast
the waiter	þjóninn	procure	útvega
some water	vatn	recommend	mæla með
hot water	heitt vatn	remain	vera eptir
cold water	kalt vatn	rest	hvíla
watch	úr	ride	ríða
wine	vín	row	róa
a bottle of wine	flösku af víni	skate	fara á skautum
port wine	portvín	speak	tala
sherry	sérrí	swim	synda
claret	rauða vín	stay	dvelja
		stop	standa við
		tell me	segja mér
III. Will you	Vilið þér	walk	ganga
ask	spyrja, biðja		
assist me	hjálpa mér	**IV. Does the**	
bring	færa, bera		
call me	kalla á mig	bell ring?	hringir bjallan?
come	koma	coach go to A?	fer vagninn til A?
drive	aka		
divide	skipta	coach stop at B?	stendur vagn-
do	gjöra		inn við í
do me	gjöra fyrir mig		B?
fetch	sækja	– stop here?	stendur vagn-
find	finna		inn við
get	fá		hérna?
go to	fara til	– leave at?	fer vagninn
away	fara burtu		burt?
from	fara frá	– take pass-	tekur vagninn
give me	gefa mér	engers?	við ferða-
go with	fara með		mönnum?
go on	fara áfram	coach start at?	fer vagninn á
hand me	rétta mér		stað?

8*

road lead to?	{liggur vegur- inn til?	*V. Is it?*	**Er hann** (það)
- take to?			
- pass near?	liggur vegurinn nærri?	attentive	aðgætinn
- crosses at?	liggur vegurinn yfirum	bad	vondur
		beautiful	fagur
railway go to?	liggur járn- brautin	bitter	bitur
		black	svartur
train go quick?	fer járnbrautar- lestin hart?	blue	blár
		blunt	sljór
train go slow?	fer járnbrautar- lestin hægt?	bold	djarfur
		broad	breiður
mail start	fer pósturinn af stað?	brown	brúnn
		careless	skeytingarlaus
journey take long?	varir ferðin lengi?	cheap	ódýr
		clean	hreinn
steamer start from?	fer gufuskipið frá?	clever	lipur
		cold	kaldur
steamer pass here?	fer gufuskipið hérna framhjá?	dark	dimmur
		dear	dýr
steamer stops here?	stendur gufu- skipið hérna við?	deep	djúpur
		disagreeable	óþægilegur
		difficult	erfiður
steamer stop at?	stendur gufu- skipið við í?	dirty	óhreinn
		dry	þurr
steamer land passengers?	lætur gufuskip- ið ferða- menn á land?	easy	auðveldur
		empty	tómur
		false	ósannur
		far	langt
way lead over?	liggur vegurinn yfir?	fine	fallegur
		flat	flatur
way lead through?	liggur vegurinn gegnum?	full	fullur
		green	grænn
way go right?	liggur vegurinn til hægri?	good	góður
		great	mikill
- - left?	liggur vegurinn til vinstri?	grateful	þakklátur
		grey	grár
- - strait on?	liggur vegurinn beint áfram?	hard	harður
		heavy	þungur
time admit of?	leyfir tíminn.	healthy	heilnæmur, heilsugóður
		high	hár

hollow	holur	*short*	stuttur
honest	ráðvandur	*sick*	sjúkur
hot	heitur	*small*	lítill
kind	góður	*soft*	mjúkur
large	stór	*sour*	súr
left	leifður, eptir	*strong*	sterkur
light	léttur	*stupid*	heimskur
long	langur	*sweet*	sætur
low	lágur	*tedious*	leiðinlegur
mild	mildur	*thick*	þykkur
narrow	þröngur	*thin*	þunnur
near	nærri	*tired*	þreyttur
new	nýr	*true*	sannur
nice	nettur	*uggly*	ljótur
obliging	greiðvikinn	*unhealthy*	óheilnæmur
old	gamall	*unwell*	ófrískur
polite	kurteis	*warm*	heitur
poor	fátækur, vesall	*weak*	veikur
prudent	hygginn, for-	*well*	heilbrigður
	sjáll	*wet*	votur
red	rauður	*white*	hvítur
rich	ríkur	*wild*	viltur
right	réttur	*wide*	viður
ripe	þroskaður	*wise*	vitur
rough	ósléttur	*wrong*	rangur
round	kringlóttur, sí-	*yellow*	gulur
	valur	*young*	ungur
sharp	skarpur		

VI. Adverbs.

all	alls	*by all means*	fyrir alla muni
almost,	næstum	*by no means*	fyrir engan mun
already	þegar	*by and by*	við og við, bráð-
always	alltaf		um
at last	að síðustu	*certainly*	vissulega
at once	í einu, undir-	*daily*	daglega
	eins	*early*	snemma
because	af þvíað	*else*	annars
besides	auk	*enough*	nóg
but	en	*ere*	áður

ever	jafnan, ætíð	*out*	út
extremely	mjög	*perhaps*	ef til vill
exceedingly,	einstaklega	*pretty*	fallegt
here	hér	*quite*	alveg
hither	hingað	*scarce*	valla
hourly	hverja stund	*seldom*	sjaldan
how	hvernig, hversu	*since*	síðan
however	samt sem áður	*so*	svo
if	ef	*some*	nokkuð
in	í	*sometimes*	stundum
indeed	svo	*soon*	bráðum
in fact	í raun réttri	*surely*	vissulega
in this manner	svona	*then*	þá
in short	í stuttu máli	*there*	þar
just now	einmitt núna	*thither*	þangað
late	seint	*thus*	þannig
like	líkt	*till*	þangað til
monthly	mánaðarlega	*to-day*	í dag
much	mikið	*to-morrow*	á morgun
neither-nor	hvorki-né	*to-night*	í kvöld
never	aldrei	*truly*	sannarlega
no	nei	*well*	vel
no doubt	efalaust	*very*	mjög
not	ekki	*where?*	hvar?
not at all	alls ekki	*whence?*	hvaðan?
nothing	ekkert	*why?*	því?
now	nú	*with*	á meðan
of course	sjálfsagt	*without doubt*	efalaust
only	einungis	*yearly*	árlega
oft	opt	*yesterday*	í gær
once	einusinni	*yet*	enn, ennþá
over	yfir		

VII. Voyage to Iceland.

I go to Iceland	eg fer til Íslands
When?	hvenær?
to-morrow	á morgun
how?	hvernig?
by the steamer from Grange-	með gufuskipinu frá Grange-
mouth,	mouth,

It is a screw steamer	það er skrúfugufuskip,
It comes from Copenhagen	það kemur frá Kaupmannahöfn,
And goes to Reykjavik	og fer til Reykjavíkur;
calls at Grangemouth	það kemur við í Grangemouth
On their outward and home-ward voyage	á út- og heim-leiðinni,
six times a year	sex sinnum á ári.
The ship is clean and fast	Skipið er hreint og traust.
The danish cheer provided is ample and wholesome	Hin danska fæða, sem veitt er, er mikil og heilnæm.
No man used to luxuries	Enginn maður, vanur við sællífi,
Should make the trip	ætti að fara þá för,
Even in fine weather	jafnvel í góðu veðri.
A few Icelanders are an board	Fáeinir Íslendingar eru á skipinu
The weather is excellent	Veðrið er ágætt.
We left the Shetlands yesterday	Vér fórum frá Skotlandi í gær.
The Faroe islands are in sight	Færeyararnar eru í sýn.
Their mountains and cliffs are lofty	Fjöllin og björgin á þeim eru há.
At noon we reashed Nalsoe	Um hádegi komumst vér til Nálseyar,
From which we went to Thors-haven	þaðan fórum vér til Þórshafnar.
We leave the Faroes for Ice-land	Vér förum frá Færeyum til Ís-lands
Iceland is one-fifth larger than Ireland	Ísland er einum fimta hluta stærra en Írland
It is situated about 500 miles N. W. of Scotland	það liggur hérumbil fimm hund-ruð mílur í útnorður frá Skotlandi
The Needles of Portland Head are curious	Drangarnir við Dyrhólaey (Port-land) eru skrítnir.
We pass the singular rock called the „Mealsack" and see Rey-kianaes	Við fórum framhjá hinum sér-staklega kletti, sem kallaður er Mélsekkur, og sjáum Reyk-janes
·The horizon is so clear, that we see in the north the mag-nificent outline of the Snae-fells Jökul	Loftið er svo bjart, að vér sjáum í norðri hina tígulegu umgjörð af Snæfellsjökli;
The view is magnificent	Útsjónin er vegleg

We soon reach the bay in which lies the capital Reykjavik	Vér komumst bráðum inná flóann, þarsem höfuðstaðurinn Reykjavík liggur.
Here you will find an hotel	Þar er gestgjafa hús;
It is not a bad one	það er ekki slæmt;
But you have only a week to return by the steamer	þer hafið aðeins viku, ef þér farið aptur með gufuskipinu.
We want ponies by to-morrow for the Geysers	Við þurfum hesta á morgun til Geysis;
Early, very early!	snemma — bráðsnemma!
The Icelanders think little of time	Íslendingar hugsa eigi mikið um tímann;
It is indefinite,	það er oákvarðað.
Early in Iceland, is at any time during the forenoon	Snemma á Íslandi er allt til hádegis.
The beds are delicious	Rúmin eru inndæl;
This is the land of eider-down	þetta er æðardúns land.
The winter requires warmths, rest, sleep	'A veturna þurfa menn hita, hvíld, svefn.
The harbour and Esianrange is visible	Höfnin sést og fjallgarður sá, sem kallaður er Esjan.
There is a pretty cemetery	þarna er laglegur kirkjugarður.
At its foot is the road to Bessastad	Fram hjá honum liggur vegurinn til Bessastaða.
This is the promenade of the beau monde	Hann er skemmtig öngusvið hinna ungu manna,
There is a cathedral	þarna er dómkirkja,
It contains a font by Thorwaldsen, •	þar er skírnarfontur eptir Thorvaldsen
who was of icelandic parentage.	Faðir hans var Íslendingur
At the back of the church is the Alsing, the house of parlament of the island,	'A bak við kirkjuna er er hús það, sem Alþing Íslands er haldið í.
But the whole town looks more like a village.	Allur bærinn lítur út líkt og þorp.
Society here is purely Danish.	Samkvæmin eru hér með alveg dönsku sniði.
The great natural phenomena, with the exception of the Krabla, lie in and about the south-west portion of the island.	Hin miklu nátturu einkenni· eru öll í og kringum suð-vestur hluta landsins, að Kröflu undan skildri.

The island is volcánic.
At Thingvalla, of historic renoun, is good shooting.

It is one of the most wonderful sights in the world.
All are riding ponies.
No one thinks of walking here.

The Salmon fishing is excellent sport,
Particularly the salmon rivers at Bogar Fiord.
From here you can go to Snaefells Jökul
Visit the valley of Reykholt and its terminal waters,
The cave of Surtshellir,
Than, if you have time, go across country to Geyser and Hekla.
Generally the visitors only go to the Geysers and Hekla.
You ought to have good travelling books.

Landið er fullt af eldfjöllum.
'A Þingvöllum, sem nafnfrægir eru í sögulegu tilliti, er nóg að skjóta.
Þeir er ein hin undrunarverðasta sjón í heimi.
Allir ríða á hestum.
Engum dettur í hug að ganga hér.
Laxveiði er ágæt skemmtun,

einkum í laxánum í Borgarfirði.
Héðan má fara til Snæfellsjökuls
Skoðið Reykholtsdalinn og laugarnar þar.
Surtshellir
Ef þér hafið þá tíma til, getið þér farið yfir um landið til Geysis og Heklu.
Vanalega fara ferðamenn aðeins til Geysis og Heklu.
þér ættið að hafa góðar ferðabækur.